W. Heimburg

A Poor Girl

W. Heimburg

A Poor Girl

ISBN/EAN: 9783744790949

Printed in Europe, USA, Canada, Australia, Japan

Cover: Foto ©Andreas Hilbeck / pixelio.de

More available books at **www.hansebooks.com**

A POOR GIRL

BY

W. HEIMBURG

TRANSLATED BY ÉLISE L. LATHROP

WITH PHOTOGRAVURE ILLUSTRATIONS

NEW YORK

WORTHINGTON COMPANY

747 BROADWAY

1892

A POOR GIRL.

I.

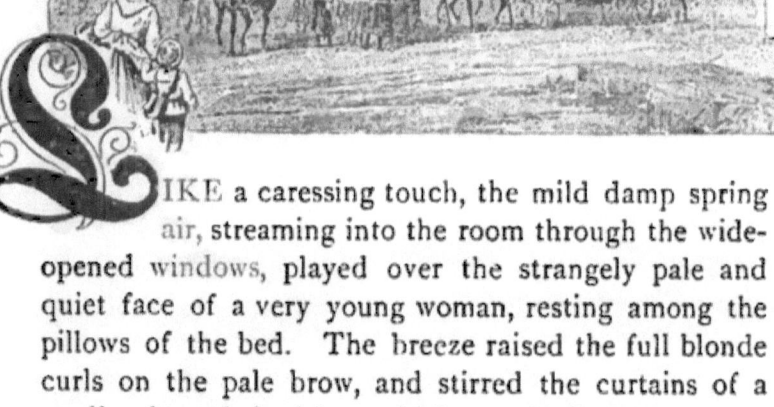

IKE a caressing touch, the mild damp spring air, streaming into the room through the wide-opened windows, played over the strangely pale and quiet face of a very young woman, resting among the pillows of the bed. The breeze raised the full blonde curls on the pale brow, and stirred the curtains of a cradle draped in blue, which, as if it were every-where in the way, had been pushed into the furthest corner of the room.

"Stand up, Hegebach," said a woman's deep voice. "God gives and God takes away, and we must bear it patiently."

She was a tall stout woman, in the forties, who with

these words approached the man who lay motionless beside the bed, and had thrown his **arms over** the dead **woman as if** in wild grief. **He did not move now, and the** speaker hastily wiped **a couple of tears from her bright** intelligent **eyes.**

"Hegebach, you must not, you cannot lie here the whole day without food and drink. Come," she continued, her reproving tone ending in a half-suppressed sob, "come, Hegebach, you still have duties—think of the child ! "

He groaned and rose. He was a man no longer young, and grief made **his** bearded face **with** the unmistakably military **cut of hair,** appear much older ; his eyes stared almost uncannily at the peaceful sweet face which slumbered there so calmly. Then turning away **abruptly,** he left the room, with **clanking spurs, no** longer a mourner, but as one enraged, **deeply** insulted. **The woman left behind straightened the white coverlet over the corpse, and smoothed the childish** face **caressingly, then brought the cradle from the** corner and carried **it out.**

In **the opposite room** something cried ; she hastily opened **the** door and entered a small one-windowed room, evidently that of the dead woman. It was indescribably dainty, although almost **too** simple **for a lady** of rank, with its white hangings **and the work-table by** the window, through which **one could look out into the** garden where the young tender green **twigs swung in** the mild **spring zephyrs.** There was no one in the room,

only on the sofa a little white bundle, from which a pair of tiny red fists protruded, and which emitted a helpless cry.

The tall stately woman suddenly fell upon her knees before the sofa, and weeping hid her face in the small cushions. "Yes, yes," she whispered, "the world does not smile upon you, you poor thing! No mother, no mother! And your father acts as though God had deeply insulted him in sending him a poor little girl. Foolish little wight, why were you not a boy? And every one gone, of course! They leave you here to cry, and you are hungry, too."

She paused and gazed for a moment, as though pondering, at the tiny puckered red face. "Wait, wait," said she, quickly raising the child. "I will take you with me to the castle; what can he do with such an atom?"

Two days later the young Mrs. von Hegebach was buried. Her short life was the talk of the day all over the little city, and those who had not known her, soon learned that she had been a penniless girl and had married the man so much her senior, and also without fortune, for the sake of a home. No one had believed it possible that he would ever marry; he had been already an old bachelor, and surly and irritable besides. Now it was just a year since this sunbeam had entered his house—what a short happiness!

"If it really was one," said many. Captain von Selchow assured several younger comrades, on the way to the funeral, that he knew from authentic sources that Hegebach's marriage had been a *coup de désespoir*. He, Hegebach, some fifteen months before, had received from his wealthy old uncle, the Bennewitzer, a letter which informed him briefly and explicitly that the uncle had no idea of leaving his fortune to a pair of old bachelors, such as, unfortunately, both his nephews were ; he wished to know for whom he had saved and cared. Whichever of the two men first announced to him the birth of a son and heir should be the chosen one. Daughters were not to be considered. Hegebach's cousin, of the Fifteenth Dragoons, had not answered this letter ; there was a rumor of an affair from which he could not at once disentangle himself. But our Captain a week later answered very laconically with the notice of his betrothal, *voilà tout*. The rest the gentlemen knew ; to-day they attended the sad conclusion of the story. " She was a charming woman, the little Hegebach—a great pity," he concluded, pathetically.

Mrs. von Ratenow of the castle had cared for the young mother, and made the arrangements for the funeral ; there was a slight relationship between them. The parents of the deceased were no longer living, but the guardian had come to the burial early this morning. Hegebach's comrades had appeared, and the regimental band had preceded the flower-laden coffin through the winding lanes, and played hymns. The widower followed the hearse in his full uniform; his rigid face ex-

pressed no grief, but rather misanthropy; it even seemed
as if the lips under the full beard, already half gray,
curled in a scornful smile.

Then that was over. The people had gone. One
more fresh mound rose in the churchyard, and the
street before the house of mourning was again deserted;
a single carriage still waited before the door, a carriage
drawn by a magnificent pair of horses, evidently belong-
ing to wealthy people.

In the dead wife's room the little basket cradle with
the sleeping child was rocked softly; an old servant,
her hands in her lap, sat beside it, with eyes red from
weeping. She had draped the simple furniture in
sheets; the dainty little table, the flowers at the window,
had vanished, as had curtains and rugs; it looked deserted and uninhabited, as though the owner had gone
on a long journey.

Mrs. von Ratenow entered the Captain's gloomy
unhomelike sitting-room. She wore hat and cloak.
" Good-by, Hegebach!" said she. " I must go home
now; they have just sent for me. Moritz has come
and things have gone at sixes and sevens at home this
week. I need not assure you that the little child will
be well cared for."

He had stood at the window and stared out into the
narrow street; now he turned and gazed in astonishment
at the resolute, still beautiful woman.

" Yes," she continued, " it needs care and attention,
Hegebach. A baby could not thrive here in your

smoky rooms. I do it for its mother's sake, for I am no longer accustomed to little children—Moritz is twenty years old."

" I thank you, dear madam," he murmured ; "indeed —I did not know——"

" Oh, no matter, dear Hegebach ; I should merely like to beg you not to be angry with the poor little creature because you will not receive that sand-hill, Bennewitz. ' Man proposes, God disposes ; ' who knows how it may all turn out ? "

" My cousin marries next month, my dear madam."

"Well, let him marry," was the answer. " If the much-longed-for son is born to him, the estate and inheritance are his, that we have long known."

" And the child ! " he cried, for the first time letting his wild grief burst forth, and tearing open his uniform. "If it were not I, Lisa would still be alive ; were it not I, a son would have cried in the cradle ! Who am I to dare stretch out my hand for happiness ? "

" Hegebach ! " said Mrs. von Ratenow, reproachfully.

" A girl without fortune," he murmured with indescribable bitterness ; " what that means in our rank in the present time you know as well as I."

" Bad enough, to be sure. But she will get along as do other poor girls—she must learn to work ; has two dear little sound hands, and two bright eyes. What shall her name be ? " she finished calmly. " Shall she have her mother's name, Elizabeth ? "

He nodded, and turned to the window again.

"Good-by, Hegebach. Will you not at least see the little thing once?"

He pressed his forehead against the window-pane, and made a hasty gesture of dissent.

"Well, then, I hope that this child may yet prove a blessing from God to you, Hegebach—that you will thank Him on your knees for the consolation sent you in your old age. May that be your reward!"

She went to the dead wife's room, the flush of excitement on her face.

"Take the child, Susan; we will set out now."

And followed by the old woman, who carried the infant, its face carefully wrapped in a blue veil, she got into the carriage.

They had no long distance to drive—down the street, past the old court-house, which still bore on its walls the traces of the thirty years' war in the form of iron cannon balls, through several winding lanes and an old gate which must date back to the middle ages, then along the city walls, over which peeped the tops of blooming fruit-trees, along a magnificent linden alley, and through a hospitably opened gate, from which the front of a high, massive building with a colossal pointed tiled roof, mossy and gray with age, was visible. And just at this moment, as the carriage rolled into the yard, the sun shed a golden light over the old brick house, which lay surrounded by lindens and ash-trees which had just put forth a light green veil of leaves on their venerable heads, as though it would give a greeting to the orphan child upon her entrance to this house, which in charity and compassion was to offer a refuge to her childhood.

The carriage stopped before the stately door, and a strikingly tall young man, evidently still in travelling garb, sprang down the steps, threw open the carriage door violently, and kissed both hands of the lady as she dismounted.

"Mother, had I suspected," he said, "but I could not possibly go to the funeral in these clothes. But what is that?" he interrupted himself, and pointed to the woman who had just alighted with the child.

"Lisa's child, Moritz. For God's sake, you will let it fall."

But the young man with the frank handsome face

had already taken the little bundle in his arms and carried it into the house, followed by the two women.

"Oh, goodness!" he cried, having reached the comfortable sitting-room, gazing tenderly as a woman at the tiny little face. "How it looks, mother; so little and twitching—my poor dear Lisa!" and he turned quickly to the window as if he did not wish it to be seen that his eyes were moist. "This is the consequence, mother," he continued; "had you not persuaded Lisa to marry that old Captain she would be living yet."

"Moritz, you are a monster," replied Mrs. von Ratenow, and she took the child from him. "Shame on you! For whom should the girl have waited? The great boy has tears in his eyes. I cannot bear to hear these laments of 'if' and 'but,' Moritz. Lisa has fulfilled her duty as a woman, let her rest."

"And the child will stay with us?"

"Certainly, Moritz," replied his mother; "where should she go?"

"That is so good of you," said he, and threw his arm around the stately woman; "good, as you alone can be."

"No nonsense, Moritz. You know that I am no sentimentalist," said she, calmly. "Your father had a tendency that way, and you have inherited it, eh? You have again spent all that money in travelling expenses so as to see your mother and your home again, you boy, you!"

She tried to look contemptuous, but she did not

succeed ; the mother-love shone **too** plainly from **her** eyes **as she** gazed at her only son.

"You have hit it, mother ; I had just time enough, and I knew that you would not be vexed."

"This confidence," said she, smiling ; "how well you know me! But **now** we will attend **to the** child. What do you think, Moritz; shall I commission Aunt Lott with her bringing up ? "

"What ? " he cried, astonished and yet amused. "Then I must be present ! Give me the young lady, I will carry her upstairs. I must witness the scene."

Aunt Lott was an adopted sister and cousin of Mrs. von Ratenow and Canoness of Z— ; but, with the exception of the prescribed eight weeks which she must spend each · year in Z—, or else forfeit her position, she lived at the castle. She was a quiet, not too intelligent creature, delicate, pale, a bit literary, and was the exact opposite of Mrs. von Ratenow, although the two had grown up together since the earliest childhood. Aunt Lott took a romantic view of everything; she lived and breathed in the poetry of the higher spheres, "high above all the dust of earth." She read everything that she could lay her hands upon, and the more touching and heart-breaking the story the more beautiful she thought it. She knew "The Enchanted Rose" by heart, and when she recited the last verse her emotion rose to the utmost height :

> "Of all that blissful time remains to me
> This song, my sufferings, and my love alone !"

This was really only sighed, not spoken.

Yes, fate had once showed her a prize—she had drawn a blank ; she had a " grave " in her heart, as she was accustomed to assure her friends.

But in spite of that the two had always been good friends. When her practical cousin married Baron von Ratenow, Lott had remained with the lonely parents, and after their death she found several pleasant rooms in the upper story of the spacious castle, in which everything was so scrupulously neat that one fairly feared to tread upon the dazzlingly polished parquet.

A purring cat sat on the window-seat behind snowy curtains; the brass doors of the tile stove shone like pure gold; a spinning-wheel stood in the corner beside the sofa, adorned with broad ribbons, and the glass cupboard was filled with all kinds of ornaments of a bygone time, chief among which was a Chinaman of Meissner porcelain, which could nod its head for hours at a time. It was enormously valuable, as Aunt Lott assured every one who admired it. She sat by the window reading a psalm; she wore a black gown and silk apron, for she had truly loved the young woman who had died after such a short life. It had been in this tidy little room that, scarcely a year ago, the girl, weeping and frightened, had laid her hand in her elderly bridegroom's, whom she had met while visiting at the castle, as the large house of the Ratenows' was called. They had played whist together, and he had been vexed when she made a mistake. A week later his sabre clanked over the castle steps; he had come *en grande tenue* to woo. He had sat in the state-room down-stairs for two hours, in suspense and anxiety, until Mrs. von Ratenow said, "Wait, Hegebach; I will bring the little girl to her senses." And she had gone up into Aunt Lott's room, where the girl crouched on a sofa, trembling and weeping, and Aunt Lott vainly strove to quiet her excited nerves with cologne and lavender, for this wooing had been like lightning from a cloudless sky to her.

After another hour she was betrothed ; the sonorous voice of the mistress of the house had been audible almost in the lowest story ; at least Moritz, who was also home on a visit, declared that he had heard such exclamations as "suitable match "—"pretensions "— ' what are you waiting for?" Into the room, where the mother had fought and struggled, Moritz von Ratenow now carried the little daughter, and, without preparation, laid it in Aunt Lott's lap.

"There, auntie, is something for the cat to be jealous of."

"Merciful heaven !" she screamed, and her eyes wandered from the child through the orderly room, and rested upon the pale, grave face of Mrs. von Ratenow.

"You have the most time, Lott ; take the child. I have brought her nurse, old Susan, with me ; you will not have much care. It could not stay with him, for it does not yet smoke cigars, and, as you know, I cannot have the care of it with all my housekeeping duties."

The old maid's delicate hands already during this speech had clasped the little bundle. She said nothing, she could not, but she nodded so energetically and affirmatively, while her face twitched and she wiped her eyes so vigorously that this could be considered a perfectly satisfactory answer. And so Moritz, at his mother's suggestion, pushed aside the cupboard which concealed a door, and when this was opened a pleasant little room, with blue chintz hangings, was seen, which had formerly been used for guests, but was now promoted to a nursery. Moritz brought the cradle upstairs, and when it grew dark Aunt Lott sat with her knitting, and near her, young Baron von Ratenow in the light from the night-lamp, beside the swinging cradle, she in a chair and he on a stool, and they spoke in whispers of the dead so eagerly that they did not notice that Mrs. von Ratenow's head appeared in the doorway, and from there she watched the strange pair. The gray cat had sprung up into the cradle and licked its paws.

"A strange boy!" murmured the mother, descending the stairs. "A man with the heart of a child—his father all over again. Of course, he does not get it from me." And she took the bunch of keys from her girdle with such energy that the girls in the kitchen, who were talking eagerly of the little child brought into the house, hurried to their work, for the mistress would brook no trifling.

So it grew up, the child, in the old house shaded by lindens, and built of and upon the ruins of a castle which had been burned down by the Swedes in the thirty years' war. A huge thick tower still stood in the garden, a wall and moat still surrounded the building, both of which were blue with violets in the spring. There was an old well, with a sweep, in the garden, a

dungeon, and eerie ghost stories by the hundred. It had long been in the possession of the Ratenows, having fallen to them through a marriage, a Ratenow having long ago wooed and won a Burgsdorf, the last of her race.

When the child's bright eyes looked out of the window, they gazed over the large yard with the stables and barns to the roofs and towers of the little city; near the tower of the court-house, under the high peaked slate roof, lived the solitary man. And when the little being, scarce two years old, was asked, "Who lives over there?" she took her little finger from her mouth and pointed and said with sparkling eyes, "Papa!"

Yes, papa; the papa who scarcely knew his child, who merely paid an occasional visit to the castle from a sense of duty, and looked at the blonde child as gloomily as though some disagreeable letter had been presented to him. And still the child met him with a cry of joy, and reached out longingly for the bright buttons of his uniform. There must be something in the little heart which made it turn unsuspectingly to the quiet, embittered man.

She was a remarkably pretty child, the darling of the whole house, great friends with Aunt Lott, the gray cat, and big Moritz. Only of Aunt Ratenow was she afraid; the rosy face became waxen at a reproving glance from this lady's bright eyes. She rushed eagerly to pick up anything that fell to the ground; but she was not as smilingly ready as with Aunt Lott, although she was no less pleasantly thanked.

"She must soon go to school," said Mrs. von Ratenow one day as she sat near the window, and her eyes
followed the child, who ran across the yard, her curls
flying out behind her, and vanished in the cow-stables,
where she was accustomed to drink her evening milk.
"She will be five years old in April," and she pushed
the spectacles, which she had worn for two years, up on
her smooth white forehead, that she might see better.

"To school?" asked Moritz, who was at home for
his Easter vacation, and was pacing up and down the
room, immensely tall and blond in his gray summer suit.
A pert little mustache covered his mouth, and his face
was as rosy as ever.

"To school?" he asked, pausing before his mother.

Mrs. von Ratenow stared at him.

"I know very well, dear mother, that she must learn
to read and write, but why not here, in the house?
There are plenty of governesses."

The work sank into his mother's lap, and her bright
eyes had an astonished expression. "Moritz, I do not
know what you are thinking of! Had I daughters of
my own I should perhaps—I say, perhaps—have selected
this aristocratic and secluded style of instruction, but
the child would be spoiled by it, and—more's the pity
—she will be soon enough."

"Then is the little thing to trot all that distance to
school, in all kinds of wind and weather? Let her at
least drive in winter, mother."

"Am I a fool, Moritz?" she replied, calmly. "If

you will guarantee her a carriage later—as far as I am concerned. Beginning with April, Elsa goes to school. How far is it? Down the carriage drive, through the stone gate into the rose alley, and—she is there!"

"It is for you to decide, mother."

"Right, my boy. And now let us speak of your plans. Well, then, when you return in the autumn from your trip to Vienna and the Tyrol, we will both reign here together, eh?"

He laughed and kissed the hand which she held out to him.

"I trust you do not yet think of marrying?" said she, suddenly, and gazed penetratingly at the young man.

"Yes, mother," he replied, coming closer to her. "I will frankly confess that I—have thought of it."

"Hear the boy! Whom have you chosen, then, child?"

"An old flame, mother dear; but do not worry yourself, she is still at boarding-school."

"Indeed! At boarding-school? What will she learn there, Moritz? She will learn to be pale and fragile, a nervous doll, so that she will never be a healthy wife and mother, and what she forgets there, you have probably not considered. All taste for a quiet family life—that will fly out the window. You should not have let her go there, Moritz, if you wish to be happy with her."

For an instant Moritz looked really abashed. That

2

his mother took the matter thus, startled and pleased him at the same time. He walked up and down the room several times, his hands behind his back ; Mrs. von Ratenow meanwhile calmly continued knitting her stocking, from time to time gazing out into the yard. This was her manner of passing the time between four and six o'clock in the afternoon—for the rest of the day she gave herself little rest.

" Hegebach intends to resign, Moritz ; did you know it ? " she asked after a while.

" It is best ; he will never be promoted," replied the son, "he quarrels with all his superior officers."

" But the small pension ? "

" Oh, well, he can live on it, mother."

" He ! He !—but the girl ? " was the impatient re-joinder.

" Oh, mother ! "

" Yes, merciful patience, Moritz—you speak of mar-rying ! When once you have half a dozen children, how do you think I shall fare ? " She had spoken jest-ingly, and both laughed.

" You dear little mother," said he, still laughing, and kissed her.

" No, joking aside," she continued, drawing back. " I take care of Elsa—you need not believe that I will half do the thing. She must learn to do something. I think she will be a governess, and I will send her to D— as soon as she is ten years old. That is the best, eh, Moritz ? "

At this moment the door opened softly, and a little head peeped into the room, with hair like molten gold; a pair of large brown eyes looked out from a rosy smiling face, and a sweet, clear, bird-like voice asked, "Moritz, Moritz, will you come into the garden with me? There is a squirrel in the chestnut-tree."

"Come here, Elsa!" cried the young man, and as the child rushed up to him, he picked her up in his arms like a doll, and carried her to his mother.

"Look at her, mother," he begged, in a strangely soft voice.

She looked in the pure childish face, and then up at him, questioningly.

"So, and now run away, Elsa, I will follow you." And the blond giant carefully opened the door to let the little girl out.

"She is as fresh, healthy and happy as a rose-bud, is she not?" he asked, returning. "And you will shut her up in a gloomy school-room during the loveliest days of her girlhood, and worry her with severe intellectual work! See, mother, I can never sleep again from thinking of it. What a world of tears and wakeful nights, of buried hopes and bitter renunciation is contained in the words, 'She must be a governess!' Ah, mother, leave her her freedom, do not shut her up, the poor little midget!"

"How you can say such a thing, Moritz, I do not understand," replied Mrs. von Ratenow impatiently, paling slightly, "as though I were about to do the child a great wrong. Do you know that she possesses nothing but three hundred dollars of her mother's, and a few trifles ? Hegebach will leave at the most debts, when he closes his eyes, and what then ? Besides, it is not so dreadful, Moritz, and for the present you need not pity your rose-bud. Because you are in love, my dear boy, I will pardon you the comparison. What ? *She* is surely a rose-bud, too," and with these words she energetically put her knitting in its basket, and left the room. And immediately after her resonant voice rang out from the cellar, " I will show you that it can be done. One can do everything that one chooses ! "

Late in the evening, Moritz von Ratenow knocked at the door of his mother's bedroom.

" I thought I heard you ride into the yard," she called from within. " Come in. Where have you been ? "

He entered, and walked cautiously up to the canopy bed. The full moon shed its light through the arched window and lit up the cosey old room so plainly.

How long it was since he had been here ! There, over the chest of drawers, hung his father's portrait, and beneath that his own picture taken when a boy. Here stood a cupboard in which his mother kept all her relics, her bridal wreath and his first little cap, his father's spurs and sword, and the last bouquet of wild flowers which he had picked for her the day before his death, and here it was again, the delicate perfume of lavender—it suddenly seemed that he was again a little boy, and came to his mother to confess some foolish act.

"What do you wish, my boy?" she asked gently, in her Bremen dialect. " Where were you?"

Suddenly he seated himself on the edge of the bed, and seized her hands. " Guess," said he, hesitatingly. " But no, you cannot guess—I was at Teesfeld—at my future father-in-law's."

"Oh, you dreadful boy!" cried Mrs. von Ratenow.

" It was only about the pension, mother; I told him that I love Frieda and she loves me, and if Mr. von Teesfeld has no objection, we will marry as——"

"And he has no objection, of course?" she inquired with an imperceptible accession of pride.

"Oh, Heaven forbid, mother? Well, in a word, Frieda is coming back from the boarding-school."

" How old is she, Moritz?"

" Sixteen and a half; Mrs. von Teesfeld thought we should wait four years yet."

"Very sensible, Moritz."

" Are you satisfied, then, mother?" he asked, softly.

"Ah, of what use would it be were I not? She is the child of good people, Moritz, in suitable circumstances, and if she is like her father, she will be a good wife." She was silent, as though pondering. " I have been too thoughtless; had I suspected that she would be my daughter-in-law—yes, yes," she continued, "it seems to me that your father once told me that Frieda was just such a fly-away as her mother. Yes, I remember distinctly. Well, listen : if such is the case, hold the reins tightly from the very first; you will have much to teach her."

He laughed. "She is sweet, mamma, just because she is such a witch."

"There is nothing to laugh at, Moritz," said she, reprovingly. "But now go to sleep. I will drive to Teesfeld to-morrow. As your mother, I must do this for your sake, eh?" And she stroked his luxuriant blonde hair. "Now go to sleep, do not gaze at the moon ; do you hear, Moritz?"

And when he had gone, she remained sitting up in bed for a long time, her hands folded. "I am glad that he is so resolute," said she at length, aloud. "When his father courted me all his friends and relatives knew of it, and the very birds sang of it on the roofs. The boy knows what he wants—he gets that from me."

II.

THE door in the old frame house whose windows overlooked the monotonous narrow street was softly opened, and the dainty figure of a little girl of probably ten years hurried in. The child wore a simple gray alpaca frock, a brown straw hat with brown ribbons, from beneath which hung two heavy pale blonde braids. In her hand she carefully held a little basket filled with pears and grapes, and in spite of her thick leather boots, she mounted the steep wooden stairs almost inaudibly, and knocked at the door upstairs.

"Come in," cried a man's voice, and the next moment Elsa von Hegebach stood in the little room filled with tobacco smoke, before her father.

He had grown very old, the man, and he looked neglected in his faded dressing-gown which he had adopted since his resignation. He had grown sallow, and the embittered expression of his face had become the predominating one. But the rosy child's face nevertheless leaned with sweet confidence against his cheek.

" Papa, how are you ?" she asked, and quickly setting the little basket down upon the table, she threw
both arms around his neck.

" Pray do not ask," was the irritable reply.

A shade fell upon the child's smiling face. " Papa,
may I stay with you for a little while ? " she asked,
shyly, " or are you going to the club ? "

" I am going to the club, you know very well, but
Susan is down-stairs."

" Dear papa"—the little rosy mouth drooped, but
the tears were suppressed bravely—" I will go down
again at once, but you know I must tell you good-by
to-day ; to-morrow I am to go to D—— "

" To-morrow ? " he asked, looking up from the paper,
" when do you leave ?"

" Mrs. Cramm said I must be at her house at seven in
the morning. Aunt Ratenow has asked Mrs. Cramm
to take me with her. Annie is going to D— also, and
because Moritz is to be married to-morrow, and they
will all be at Teesfeld, and no one can take me——"

" Oh yes," he interrupted, impatiently, " it is very
sensible so ; the term probably begins day after to-morrow ? "

"Yes, papa. Shall I read aloud to you from the
paper, papa ? "

" No, thanks ! Well, a happy journey, Elsa, and be
industrious." He held out his hand, and picked up his
newspaper again.

The child stood perfectly motionless, her pale lips

twitched slightly, but no word issued from them, only the sweet eyes gradually became staring. She turned and left the room.

"Elsa," was called after her; she started, "give those things to Susan—I never eat such." And he pointed to the dainty little basket.

Suddenly she fell on her knees before him, the irritable, unfriendly man. "Papa! papa!" she cried shrilly, "why do you not love me a little bit? Why do you never speak kindly to me as Annie's papa does?" Her whole little frame quivered in passionate excitement; she leaned her blonde head against his knee and burst into convulsive sobs.

"Dear heaven, child, pray stand up," cried old Susan, who had come in when the girl began to weep, and she raised the half-resisting child and took her in her arms, glancing severely at the Major. He had sprung up, and now walked excitedly about the room.

"Who has done anything to you?" he asked, half anxiously, half vexedly; "have you been scolded? What is the matter? Pray tell me! If you are ill Susan shall take you home and put you to bed."

"I am not ill," was the low reply. "Good-by, papa." And hastily wiping her eyes, she left the room and went into the one which formerly had been her mother's, and which Susan had occupied since she had kept house for the Major. The child quietly seated herself by the window, and gazed out into the

uncultivated garden ; she had been so sad these last
few weeks.

Then Aunt Ratenow had summoned her to her room
one day, and had told her—how was it ?

" Elsa," she had begun, smoothing the child's soft
blonde hair, "you are now ten years old, and a sensible
child, it is now time to speak with you of all sorts of
grave matters.   Listen, every one must be of some use
in life, if she wishes to be happy, and you wish to be, do
you not ?   Many people are born, so to say, with a
silver spoon in their mouths, and need have no cares in
their whole lives, need not ask, ' What shall we eat, what
shall we drink, how shall we be clothed ? '   Others, during their whole lives, must repeatedly ask themselves
these questions, and that is not the worst by far, for the
Bible says, 'A man's life consisteth not in the abun-
dance of things which he possesseth.'   Your father,
Elsa, is a sickly, lonely man, who has borne much in
this life, and he is a poor man—he cannot give you a
silver spoon.   But instead of this, the good God has
given you good sense, and a healthy, strong body, and
it will be easy for you to answer the questions of which
I just spoke, if you have the honest will.   I should like
to impress it upon you to be very good and diligent,
Elsa, so that you will pass your governess's examinations
well ; this is almost the only path which a young lady
of rank has before her, if she must stand on her own
feet in the world."

It seemed to the child that suddenly a dark veil was

thrown over the modest pleasures of her whole life. The gray-school room appeared before her eyes, with the close atmosphere, the walls which seemed to crush her, the windows through which so seldom a sunbeam fell. And she was to be shut up in this room, she who loved flowers, air and sunlight so greatly ; shut up not only until she were grown—no, forever, forever ! But that was impossible !

" Well, Elsa, are you not pleased ? "

She not only shook her head—the whole delicate frame quivered with dread.

" Then remain a little stupid, then you will be like Susan, and one who has learned nothing will be treated like her."

" But why should I ? " she had cried ; " all the other girls need not ! " And the large fawn-like eyes gazed up into the stately woman's grave face, as if there seeking the solution of an incomprehensible riddle.

" Oh, many must, Elsa, and you among them. It is my duty to educate you so that you can be independent. Now go ; you know you must be obedient, Elsa, even if you do not now see why."

Then she had gone to Aunt Lott, pale and with hurried breath. " I am to go away, aunt ! " She could say nothing else then, and her gaze had wandered over the comfortable room, and remained fixed upon the good old face. Then she had seen two tears roll down the wrinkled cheeks upon the cap-strings, and she had been so frightened that she could not cry.

She was to go away for such a very long time, away
from her childhood's home, from the shady garden,
from Moritz, from all.   And yesterday Aunt Lott had
packed her trunk with many tears, and she had taken
leave of her, of Aunt Ratenow, and of dear, dear Moritz,
for they had all gone to Teesfeld yesterday to the wedding.   Aunt Lott had taken down her gray silk gown
from the closet, and had even mounted her Pegasus
for the solemn occasion.   Elsa knew the poem by heart;
it had a decided resemblance to the "Enchanted Rose,"
and there was a great deal about love, chains of
roses, and the magic of love.   Oh, it must be so pleasant
to go to a wedding.   She would have so liked to go,
but Aunt Ratenow had not permitted it on account of
the journey.   "What would you do there, Elsa?" she
had said; "children are only in the way."

She had been alone all day, even the cat had gone to
take a walk upon the roof.   What comfort was it to her
that at noon the maid brought her a glass of wine and
a piece of cake for dessert?   "From the young master,
Elsa; he impressed it upon me," she had said.   But for
the first time Elsa felt the pangs of loneliness—the hot,
deep longing for a heart which belonged wholly to her,
to which she had a sacred right.   And then she had
run to papa.

Now she sprang up suddenly—she could stay no
longer in the small, unhomelike room.   It smelled of
bad coffee, there were grease-spots upon the floor, and
on the wall hung the old woman's entire wardrobe; the

simple mahogany furniture was dulled and the sofa covering moth-eaten and shabby. She ran down the stairs as if chased, hurried through several streets, and then stood in the church-yard, panting for breath, before the ivy-covered mound of the mother she had never known.

The September day was drawing to a close; dark clouds had gathered in the west, and the evening breeze cooled the tear-stained childish face. And so she sat there until the sexton's wife chanced to pass her, and called to her pleasantly that she must go now, for the church-yard was to be closed at once.

She hastily picked a few ivy leaves before she left the grave. And then she stood by the window in Aunt Lott's cheerful room and listened to the singing and laughter of the maids and grooms, who celebrated their master's .wedding with punch until far into the night.

When on the following morning the sun slowly broke through the clouds about eight o'clock, it shone upoh a child's pale face, whose large questioning eyes peeped out of the window of a carriage which was rolling rapidly along the highway. On the back seat sat a round comfortable looking woman in a black velvet mantle, and a corpulent little man, while between them was their daughter, a snub-nosed child with straw-colored hair. They were taking her to the famous old D— institute for a couple of years. Each parent held one little hand, and the mother's eyes showed plainly how bitterly she had wept. Elsa sat alone on the front seat with the luggage, and to the child the un known strange life in which her little feet had to-day taken the first steps looked gloomy and hard.

III.

EIGHT years had elapsed since that time, and had left their traces on the inhabitants of the little city.

Major von Hegebach still sat in his ugly sitting-room smoking and reading, old Susan still made her dreadful coffee, but the Major no longer went so regularly to the club; it was hard for him to walk, he limped. Fatal gout had deprived him of the only diversion which he now possessed, and his temper was not improved thereby. Old Susan had a harder time than ever, but she did not think so, for she had grown stupider, and except her coffee-pot, scarcely anything in the world interested her—Elsa, perhaps, excepted.

Regularly every four weeks had a letter been laid upon the old man's writing-desk, and the handwriting had gradually changed from a childish scrawl to a fine elegant woman's writing, not without character. He had answered but one; that was when Elsa was confirmed, and then with the letter had come a garnet necklace, the only ornament which her dead mother had possessed.

A tender thankful letter had come in reply, with the

childish promise always to be an obedient daughter to
her dear papa. And now, to-day, a little note again lay
before him.

MY DEAR, REVERED PAPA :

You shall be the first to learn that I have passed my examination A. No. 1 ! The principal just sent for me to tell me. I am
so glad and happy, all my pains are forgotten. Now I shall come
in a few days, my dear papa, and I shall be glad with all my heart
to see you again.   Your loving daughter,   ELSA.

He had read the letter again and again, and his face
grew more and more grave as he did so. And while he
brooded over it, an old woman's two hands up in the
castle were busy preparing the room for the child who
was to return home. Aunt Lott and Aunt Ratenow
had received the same joyous news by the second post,
and the first had immediately set about rearranging the
young girl's former nursery, for of course she would
occupy this room again.

Down in old Mrs. von Ratenow's sitting-room nothing
had changed in the course of years, only she herself
had grown somewhat stouter, and her face expressed
perhaps more plainly unbending will and quick, ener-
getic activity. And yet there was something new here
which lent the comfortable room with the soft carpet,
the heavy blue hangings, and the shining old bronze
ornaments an indescribably home-like, cosey character.
Before the chimney, in which a fire flickered, crouched
three children playing, a boy and two girls, two blonde

blue-eyed maidens, with the rosy complexion of their father, whom they strikingly resembled, and a dark little rogue of a boy—the youngest. There were noise and laughter here which would have pained the ears of any one but a grandmother. Mrs. von Ratenow, nevertheless, seemed not to hear ; she was reading a letter, let it sink, and then read on again.

"Lulu," cried she, "run and bring papa to me."

The eldest, a slender girl of five, sprang up and ran quickly out of the room. A little while after a small, indescribably dainty little woman, dressed entirely in elegant black, fairly floated under the blue portières, and was greeted by the children with loud cries, "Mamma, mamma ! "

"You dear little things," said she, kissing the children, and then to Mrs. von Ratenow, with eager curiosity, "Moritz is coming at once, mamma—what is it ?"

"Is your name Moritz, little curiosity ?" said she, not unpleasantly, but also not very encouragingly.

But the little creature would not be frightened away; she threw her arms around the old lady's neck with a laugh.

"Oh, dear mamma, you know that I am frightfully curious; it surely is not a state secret. Please, please, let me stay ! "

"Will you ever be sensible, Frieda? Will you always remain a child ? But that is what comes of it, because Moritz spoils you so terribly."

She had been made to be indulged, this charming

3

little person with the dainty frame, the delicate oval face, and the shining blue-black hair which, arranged simply, displayed the beautiful shape of the head, with the large deep blue eyes under long black lashes. No wonder that "the boy," as his mother called him, was as much in love to-day as in the first days of his married life.

"Of course," said he, entering the room, speaking as though vexed, but with sparkling eyes, "here she is to learn what it is all about."

"I know nothing yet, Moritz."

"That is certainly very sad, little wife. Hush, you romps," cried he, holding his ears. "Who can speak a word here? Go down-stairs to Caroline."

The mother had meanwhile handed her son the letter.

"Elsa has passed her examinations and is coming Thursday," she remarked.

"Ah, really!" cried the stately man, pleased. "Well, thank goodness, she will be glad to be able to turn her back on the school-room."

"I merely wished to ask you, Moritz, what is to become of her now?"

His honest kind eyes gazed at her in astonishment. "Nothing at all for the present, mamma. I think the poor thing must have a rest first ; she will need some recreation."

Mrs. von Ratenow nodded. "Very good. But you make her return to her father's house so much the harder."

"Yes, Moritz, you will only spoil her by that," cried the young wife in assent.

"Mercy! The poor child! Why should she have anything to do with the old polar bear?" came from the man's lips, compassionately.

"It is her duty to tend her old father; the man fairly starves, Moritz; Susan grows older and dirtier every day."

"Yes, you are right, mother," he interrupted her, "but not just yet; we have time enough to consider that. The house down there must at least be so repaired that it is a fit home for human beings. Had I suspected it I should have attended to it long ago, but I will not take the girl there as it is now. The first two weeks she will spend here; do not attempt to dissuade me."

"Here we are again on the same spot," said the old lady.

"And on the right one, mother."

A short pause ensued, during which only the click of the knitting-needles was heard.

"It is two years ago to-day since the accident happened to the Bennewitzer's two sons," began the young man at length. "It is fearful to lose two children at once."

"Heavens, yes, it is horrible," chimed in the young wife. "I do not understand even to-day how it could happen."

"Very simply, Frieda. The two boys had gone out

sailing alone on the Elbe, and a sudden gust of wind must have capsized the boat; the corpses were not found until the following day."

"Yes, that is hard," remarked Mrs. von Ratenow, and involuntarily dried her forehead with her handkerchief.

"It is also just four years ago that his wife died !"

Suddenly she let her hands fall in her lap and stared thoughtfully before her. At length she said with a deep blush, "Could not Elsa—the man is wealthy and quite alone——"

"Indeed I have thought of that," replied Moritz. "Meanwhile, as daughters are expressly excluded from inheriting, according to the will of the deceased uncle, and the Bennewitzer is not at all an old man, one can scarcely doubt that he will marry again, and——"

"'The bread falls out of the beggar's pocket again and again,' is an old proverb, my boy," Mrs. von Ratenow interrupted him, having fully recovered her self-possession, "but I must invite him here, Moritz — I found his card recently."

"Do you know the Bennewitzer Hezebach well, mamma?" asked the young wife. "I have never troubled myself about him, but my sister Lili raves over him," she continued; "he is a stately man, and certainly does not resemble his cousin. I know nothing further."

But Mrs. von Ratenow made no reply.

"Moritz," she asked, "how are the roads?"

"Good and firm, mother—the rain scarcely laid the dust."

"Then pray excuse me, I have a visit to pay." She had risen, and nodding pleasantly to the young couple, went into her adjoining bedroom.

"Where are you going, mother?" asked Moritz.

"Mamma, in a quarter of an hour I am going to Mrs. von Kayser's," cried the young lady through the crack of the door, "if you can wait that long."

"Thanks, child, I am going," was the answer. But they received no answer to the question, "Where are you going?"

It was quite dark when Mrs. von Ratenow returned, and going directly upstairs, knocked at Aunt Lott's door and immediately after entered the room. Aunt Lott sat at the window and looked out at the autumn garden. She had laid away book and knitting, the twilight had so deepened.

"No, Lott, it is incredible," cried Mrs. von Ratenow, and seated herself, out of breath, on the nearest
chair.

Aunt Lott was frightened, her cousin so seldom lost
her reserved calm manner.

"Dear Ratenow! For God's sake what has happened?" asked she, leaving the window.

"No, Lott, I have come to you because I cannot
speak with Moritz about it. What has happened?
Well, you know Elsa comes to-morrow. Moritz and
I hold different views concerning her future position.
I said she must go to her father, he said that was
horrible, she should come here——"

"And Frieda?" Aunt Lott ventured to interrupt.

"Frieda? Frieda has nothing to do with it," was
the reply in a very contemptuous tone; "she says one
thing this time, another thing another time, just as suits
her, but she has no judgment, never had any. If she
wished to have private theatricals and needed some one
for a rôle for which Elsa was adapted, she would say,
'Ah, mamma, do not let her go to her surly old father;'
and if there chanced to be thirteen at table, she would
probably have declared, 'Oh, yes, mamma, the child
belongs to her father '—merely on account of the omi-
nous number."

Mrs. von Ratenow paused for a moment.

"Well, in short," she continued, while she hastily un-
fastened her heavy silk mantle, "I dressed and went
to see Hegebach. I hoped that he would wish to have

the child in his house, so that his old days might be a trifle cheered. And what do you think, Lott?" she cried, with raised voice, and let her hand fall heavily upon the top of the table. "He does not want her! Have you ever read in any of your stupid novels of a father who did not wish to receive his only child into his house? He grew fairly violent at last, he trembled in every limb, spoke of the hundred claims of a young girl, and that he had but one—rest, rest, rest!"

"But dear Ratenow, you excite yourself more than necessary," cried Aunt Lott, trying to sooth her. "He has always been so."

"But the man should not grow angry," continued the irritated woman. "He showed me very plainly that he had no use for such an article of luxury as a grown daughter. He had scarcely what he needed for himself, he had payments to make each month on his old lieutenant debts—who would undertake that after his death? He could do no more than what he had done when he gave the three hundred dollars which Lisa had brought him for her education. Elsa might now make use of what she had learned, and so on."

"The poor girl! The poor girl!" said Aunt Lott, and drew her handkerchief across her eyes.

"But I talked to him, Lott," continued the excited lady, "and you know that my words are not honeyed."

Aunt Lott was silent, she knew that only too well.

"He became quiet and pale at last, but of what use

was it ? I meant well with him—one can force no one
to be happy——"

"And now, dear Ratenow ? "

"Well, now Moritz will have his way," was the
grumbling answer.

"Ah, let it be, cousin," said Aunt Lott kindly, whose
heart secretly rejoiced that her darling was to return,
"let it be—who knows what will happen, see——"

"I know very well, Lott," Mrs. von Ratenow interrupted her; "it will be a life of pure gayety, a spoiling in
all earnest, as is now, alas, the fashion with us, and she
must work some day, for the 'must' will come, you
may depend upon it, and perhaps at no distant time.
But then she will have forgotten to accommodate herself
and submit to others."

"Oh, that is in God's hands, dear.   She may marry."

"Will you assure her a dowry, Charlotte ?" she
asked, mockingly ; "then do not make it too small."

"Oh, this prose !" groaned Aunt Lott, insulted.

"You will not bake a single roll with your poesy, nor
once cover the table.   Every one has a stomach, my
dear, and even in the tenderest love passages one gets
hungry ; that our young men of to-day know very well,
and they know, in addition, that caviare tastes better
than barley broth."

Aunt Lott did not utter a syllable in reply to this
bitterly realistic declaration.   After a while of deepest
silence, she began again, shyly :

"Ratenow, I have an idea if you—no, if Moritz—

Frieda said the other day that she must soon have a governess. If Elsa should try her hand with the children, she would then have a serious occupation, and——"

She paused anxiously and tried to see the features of the woman sitting opposite her, in the deep twilight.

"That is—perhaps that would do, Lott," said Mrs. Ratenow, and rose. "That really is not a bad idea, Lott—I will speak to Moritz at once."

She picked up her mantle and hung it over her arm.

"I will tell you, Lottie," she said, turning at the door, "I am very anxious to keep the child near me, and she will not be exactly a governess—but do not let her notice it. Good evening, Lott!"

And then the door closed, and the firm tread echoed from the corridor, and Aunt Lott stood in the middle of the quiet little room, shaking her head. Oh, this world becomes more and more prosaic!

IV.

A DREARY, disagreeable Octobei day was drawing to a close. The locomotive, a long train of cars behind it, rushed through the heavy gray fog, its red eyes glowing, and blew mighty clouds of smoke into the white sea of vapor, and now fog and smoke whirled and curled in wild, fantastic forms, they clung to the branches of the trees, ever giving place to new ones, incessantly rushing madly on.

At the window of the ladies' carriage stood a young girl, so tall and slender that the ribbon of her round straw hat was almost as high as the lower sash of the window. She was the only occupant of the coupé this cold, wet autumn evening, but her young face expressed no sense of cold and loneliness, her cheeks glowed in happy expectation, the brown fawn-like eyes shone, her full little mouth wore a half smile, or remained open for a moment, as if in expectation of something wonderful, which lent the face a sweet childlike expression. She walked from one window to another, but she could see nothing but smoke, and the train went unbearably slowly she thought. Probably for the twelfth time she picked up her travelling bag and laid it down again.

How astonished they all would be! Moritz expected her at ten o'clock, and now it was only seven.

Her heart beat to bursting when the locomotive gave a long shrill whistle, and now a few lights rushed past the windows. How long it was since she had been here! For the last year and a half it had never been convenient for her to pass her holidays at the castle— once they were all away, then the children had the measles.

Ah, and there lay the railway station! Elsa raised the window and leaned far out into the cold, damp autumn air. There stood the fountain, there stood the old one-eyed porter, and down there, across the fields, the lights of the little city shone through the mist and fog. Ah, how delightful it is to come home again!

"Where to, Miss?" asked the porter.

"Oh, let it stay; it will be sent for to-morrow from the castle," said she hastily, "I have come sooner—— "

"Will you go alone?" The man was desperate at thought of earning nothing.

Elsa remembered that Aunt Ratenow had always thought it unsuitable for ladies alone. "You may carry my bag, but quickly, please." And she hurried on ahead, along the well-known sparsely built-up road, to the city gate, and only here did her panting companion overtake her. There it stood, the old court-house; there they were, the tall crooked houses, and the lanterns still hung on chains across the streets, the knockers still rattled on the house-doors, and the shops where Moritz had sometimes bought her candy had the same darky boy figures behind their windows, as a sign that genuine tobacco was for sale here.

At length she stood still and gazed up at a pair of dimly-lighted windows; involuntarily she turned to the door to hurry to papa. But Moritz had expressly written that he and Aunt Ratenow wished to speak with her first—no, she must be obedient, and slowly she turned.

"You have gone far out of your way, Miss," grumbled her companion. "You surely do not know the right direction."

She merely nodded with a smile and walked on hastily through the stone gate into the linden alley. She knew every one of the gnarled trunks, which rose like black forms in the darkness; she remembered the lantern down there and the barking of the dogs in the castle yard which she now heard. She stood at the turn of the road. There it lay before her, the dear old house; up there were Aunt Lott's windows— they were bright—and below those in Aunt Ratenow's room; the lights burned over the house door, and behind the kitchen windows figures were moving, and the large carriage was being brought out of the barn.

"You can go," she whispered to the man, taking the bag and pressing some money into his hand. She ran across the yard, rushed up the steps, and now stood in the vestibule.

Where should she go first? But she hesitated for a moment only, then turned to the stairs and mounted to the neat little room. It was her dearest, best home. "Aunt Lott!" she cried, upon the threshold. It rang through the strange old lady's quiet room.

"Elsa! my darling child!" was the reply. Yes, she

was home again. Here she was expected. Ah, it is too lovely to come home, to come home from among strangers !

" Merciful patience ! I scarcely recognized you, Elsa, only your eyes are the same ! " cried Aunt Lott, after she had released the girl from her arms.

" Darling auntie, I have grown, have I not ? But I am eighteen years old."

" Come, come, take off your jacket, so—and here, do you see, tea is just ready. To be sure, eighteen years old, my child ? I have told you in the poem for your birthday what that means for us." And Aunt Lott stood with the teapot in her hand, before the smiling rosy girl, and declaimed :

> " Eighteen years old ! spring's magic charm
> Is thine for these brief days,
> Half unclosing fairest rosebuds
> Kissed by the sun's warm rays."

" Oh, auntie, and I so love life ! " the girl interrupted the old lady. " When I sat over my books, and my head was so heavy that it seemed as if I could cram nothing more into it, then I thought of all the happiness which must come to every one, of the youth which lay before me. Sister Beata always told us that Heaven grants a share of happiness to each one. Ah, aunt, how I look forward to my share! I could scarcely wait to leave the school-room."

Aunt Lott hastily poured tea ; she was suddenly in the midst of a dream of spring and the song of nightingales, she also had once been young, and there sat the embodiment of spring in her little room. How pretty Elsa had grown ; the young face gazing out into life was fresh as the dew ; how many, many hopes were hidden behind the smooth white forehead, and brightened the eyes and made glad the heart !

" O youth ! " whispered the old lady.

" Eighteen years old ! The poorest life
Yet has its pleasures bright,
Filling the future's gloomy vales
With golden, glad sunlight."

And there she sat, now, the girl. She had worked hard for years, she had no home, no loving mother, no prospects for the future, and still youth, which looks upon it as its right to be happy, to demand happiness, raised her to a true heaven, and how long would it last before Aunt Ratenow would come with her garden shears, and in her horribly realistic manner, cut off one bud of hope after another ? Aunt Lott turned away to set the tea-pot on the stove, so that she could become mistress of her grief.

" But, auntie, how are you all here ? " cried Elsa, quickly drinking her tea. " I must go down-stairs to Aunt Ratenow, Moritz, and Frieda."

" Yes, that you must, child, yes, yes," said the old woman. " To be sure you will not see much of Frieda ; they are having a rehearsal, they wish to play some piece for Aunt Ratenow's birthday, but Moritz will probably have a few minutes to spare."

"Rehearsal!   Who?"

"Who?   Child, the officers and young ladies from
the city, and then they are all to have supper here—
day before yesterday they even had a dance.   Mercy!
Elsa, I hear your aunt's step, and now you did not go
to see her first."

"No, that is Moritz!" cried Elsa, and in a moment
she was behind the stove, and drew her gown tightly
around her slender form.

Yes, it was Moritz; he merely wished to ask whether
Aunt Lott would drive to the station for the child.
Frieda again had the whole town down-stairs to supper.
With these words he sank down upon the nearest chair,
and pushed his hair back from his forehead, a gesture
which was frequent with him when he wished to drive
away unpleasant thoughts.

Then suddenly two trembling little hands were laid
over his eyes. "Uncle Moritz, who am I?" asked a dear,
well-known voice, and a clear, merry laugh followed.

"You witch!" he cried, and held her fast. And now
he sprang up. "Girl, you have become a fine creature!"   His good face fairly shone. "The food in
D—— cannot be very poor, in truth, and you do not
look learned either, thank God!"

"No, Moritz, I have no tendency that way.   Imagine,
the Professor assured me only yesterday that such was
the case," said she, meekly.   "But the examination went
finely," she added, consolingly, as he watched her, smilingly.

He still stared at her. "Aunt Lott, I am growing old. I have often carried that tall young lady, and now?"

"Yes," cried Aunt Lott. "When I saw her thus before me so suddenly, I thought of Schiller's words:

"'And gracefully, in beauty's pride, like to some heavenly image fair.'"

"That is right, Lott," a voice interrupted her. "Put ideas in her head at once." Aunt Ratenow stood in the doorway as if conjured there by magic, and behind her Frieda's face peeped in, wreathed in smiles.

"We wished to see if it were true," she cried.

"Caroline declared that she heard Elsa talking up here; truly, there she is."

Elsa had just emerged from Aunt Ratenow's double shawl, which the old lady was accustomed to wrap around her when passing through the cold corridors. Now she was kissed warmly by the younger lady. "Moritz, she comes as if sent for. I have just received a note from Mrs. von D——; she cannot take part, there has been a death in the family. Now we are provided for."

"What is it?" asked Mrs. von Ratenow, sharply.

"I have no time, dear mamma. I must go downstairs, and you must not ask me now, either," cried Frieda. "Moritz, bring Elsa down afterwards." And in the next moment the dainty young woman in the heavy, pale blue silk gown had vanished behind the door.

"Well, child," Aunt Ratenow turned to the young

4

girl, "we have decided that, for the present, you are to remain here."

"Oh, how gladly—if papa will permit," was the frank reply, "but then, aunt——"

"Yes, he *permits,*" the old lady interrupted. It sounded strangely. Aunt Lott and Moritz exchanged glances.

"And so that you——" she continued.

"We will speak of the rest to-morrow," Moritz interrupted. "Dear mother," he pleaded, "do us the pleasure to take supper with us this evening. Frieda would be very happy."

"You know, Moritz, that I cannot bear much talking," she replied.

"Dear heaven, it would be much pleasanter could we be alone together—but—ah, pray do; Aunt Lott and Elsa, get ready. Mother and Aunt Lott can excuse themselves soon after supper. Mother will really be needed."

Mrs. von Ratenow shook her head.

"My old birthday now furnishes an excuse for your foolery," said she; "come and fetch me when the time comes, Moritz."

"Aunt Lott," began Elsa, after she had completed her toilet, and was fastening a pale pink sash to her plain black cashmere gown, which was so becoming to her clear complexion and blonde hair, "things are so queer here; Aunt Ratenow was out of temper, and Moritz also."

"Yes, but—I do not know why," was the evasive reply. "Are you ready? It is high time."

Elsa was ready, and together they crossed the corridor and descended the stairs.

"Oh, Elsa, my handkerchief," cried Aunt Lott, as they were about to enter the drawing-room. She always forgot something.

"Go in, auntie, I will fetch it," said the young girl.

She came down-stairs again after a few minutes and paused irresolutely. Not far from her she perceived an officer; he had just removed hat and overcoat. Now he picked up a violin-case and turned to enter the hall leading to Frieda's rooms. At this moment he glanced up, and the two young people looked into each other's eyes.

Then what is usual when a lady and gentleman meet occurred: he made a deep bow, his spurs clicked, he opened the door, and let the young girl pass ahead.

The hall was but dimly lighted, but in crossing it Elsa had time to admire the handsome furniture which had been recently added to the large gloomy room. It had become the exact copy of an old German state apartment, with its dark oaken wainscoting, the magnificent carved oak furniture, the costly hangings, which fell in artistic folds to the ground. Here and there the light was reflected from handsome bronze ornaments, and the palms in the superb vases stirred gently as her feet trod the soft carpet.

Frieda's drawing-room was brilliantly lighted, and
gay chat and laughter rang out from it. When the

young girl appeared in the doorway the conversation ceased for a moment, introductions followed, and Elsa stood in the midst of the close, perfumed atmosphere of the drawing-room. She took refuge behind Aunt Lott, where there was a vacant chair, and from here she surveyed this gay scene, so wholly unfamiliar to her large childish eyes. How they chatted, laughed and joked, discussed the news of the day and of the little circle, promotion, and a bit of the *chronique scandaleuse*, interrupted by an occasional emphatic remark from Aunt Ratenow. There was an assemblage of dazzling uniforms, of ladies' handsome though simple costumes; and suddenly it flew from mouth to mouth, "Bernardi will play!"

The officer who had entered with Elsa took a violin from its case, and spoke eagerly to Frieda, then she seated herself at the piano, turning back the fine lace at her wrists, and struck a few chords, while death-like stillness prevailed in the room.

"Bernardi is to play. Elsa, you have a treat in store," Aunt Lott whispered to the girl; "he plays wonderfully." And the next moment from beneath the bow, guided over the strings by the man's slender hand yonder, a tone wonderfully soft and sweet vibrated through the room; tone succeeded tone, now mournful and longing, as though the little brown violin wept, now in brilliant staccato, in wild fiery rhythm. And then he lowered his bow.

Elsa started; she felt as though awakened from

a dream.   Loud applause followed, Aunt Ratenow
applauding loudest of all.

"Dear Bernardi," she cried, "I, indeed, understand
nothing of modern music.   Your father moved me to
tears when he played Beethoven's 'Adelaide' upon the
same violin ; but I must, nevertheless, give the palm to
his son."   And she held out her right hand to the young
man, cordially, who took it with a deep bow.   Then he
whispered to Frieda, and in the next moment, making a
second bow to the old lady, he raised his bow and
Beethoven's 'Adelaide' echoed through the room.

"'Plainly gleameth on every crimson petal Adelaide,
Adelaide !'" Aunt Lott whispered with shining eyes.
"Oh, what a pity, over so soon !   Oh, dear Lieutenant
Bernardi, how beautiful !" she heard Elsa say then,
and when she looked up he stood before her aunt, but
his eyes gazed over the blonde lace cap at the girl ; they
were dark, almost mournful eyes, which gave a peculiar
look to the face with its regular features and bold,
dark mustache.   His comrades declared that he was
descended from gypsies, and for this reason he could
"fiddle" so brilliantly.

"Is Miss von Hegebach also musical ?" he now
asked, as carelessly as possible, and drew his chair
between Elsa and Aunt Lott.

"I sing a little," she replied, and with that conversation was started.   Aunt Lott merely went through the
formality of interposing an occasional word ; she knew
nothing at all of music, but was secretly astonished at

this little Elsa's knowledge, she talked so learnedly of thorough-bass, Chopin, and Wagner.

She sat beside him at table, she did not realize how quickly the hours flew. She saw neither Moritz's smile nor Aunt Ratenow's stern glances. "One can take the girls of the present day from the nursery and seat them at table, and they will have something to talk about," said the old lady to herself. Then she rose and gave the signal for leaving the table. When Elsa kissed her hand and wished her *gesegnete mahlzeit* she held the young girl fast by the arm.

"You will take me to my room, eh, child?" and without awaiting Frieda's return—she was occupied in the adjoining room—she took "French leave" and left the room unnoticed by Moritz.

"So, Elsa," said she, when they had entered her comfortable room, "how these young women can chatter. Your tongue was not exactly tied. Did you amuse yourself?"

"Oh, aunt!" The young girl became crimson.

"The best was Bernardi's playing," said Mrs. von Ratenow, without noticing the blush. "Ring for the maid, Elsa; she may bring me fresh water, and then you may go. Go to bed, child; we must have a talk together to-morrow morning."

"Elsa, where are you?" cried Frieda's voice outside.

"Oh, well; do as you please," murmured the old lady. And when Frieda entered the room the next moment, she hastily motioned to Elsa to go.

"I do believe that mamma wished to send you to bed, like a little child," said the young wife, outside. "Come quickly; you must read your part to-night; afterwards we will dance."

It was long past midnight when Elsa mounted the
stairs. She gazed over the carved bannisters down into
the hall, where the guests stood wrapped in cloaks and
mantles, ready to leave. There stood Bernardi among
them and glanced up and bowed. "Good-night," she
cried, like a happy child. Then she sat on Aunt
Lott's bed for a long time, and told her of school, of
Sister Beata, and everything under the sun ; they even
spoke of the dead cat. It mattered not to her what
she talked about, for as to sleep that was not to be
thought of for this night.

V.

THE next morning the rain fell in torrents, the roofs dripped, the eaves-troughs gurgled and murmured, and the half-stripped branches of the trees bent and groaned in the cold autumn wind. This chilly mood seemed to affect human beings also; in the whole house only Aunt Lott and her little adopted daughter seemed good-tempered. "Now, auntie, you must have an easy time," the latter had said, and when the old lady entered her room she found all her little tasks finished, the dust removed, the flowers watered, the wants of the little canary in its cage attended to, and Elsa, in her simple gown, sat by the window and gazed out at the rainy landscape.

"I do so like this weather," she began, as they were drinking their coffee, "for then it is so nice in the house, but still it is unfortunate that it rains. I must go to papa. Aunt Lott, my conscience pricks me for enjoying myself so much yesterday evening, instead of being with him."

She had scarcely spoken when there was a knock, and Moritz .entered. He wore a thick frieze overcoat and high boots.

"Ah, Moritz, you have your headache face on," cried Elsa.

"I came to ask Elsa if she will go to the city with me. I have business at the city hall," he answered.

She was ready at once, and went for her cloak and hat. Moritz looked after her.

"She has grown to be a sweet, pretty girl, Aunt Lott," said he, as the door closed behind her.

The old lady eagerly nodded assent. "But how are matters down-stairs, Moritz?"

"Well, as one looks upon it! Frieda is unhappy; she has received news of the death of her father's brother. She never knew him, she says, but the family will of course wear mourning, especially as the old gentleman was unmarried and leaves his whole fortune to my father-in-law. Frieda wishes to go to the city with me to make some purchases."

"Oh, oh!" said Aunt Lott, "and the theatricals?"

"They are at an end, thank fortune," said he, smiling in spite of his headache. "Well, well, Elsa, you need not hurry so," he remarked to the young girl, as she reappeared. "Frieda is not nearly ready, but you can say good-morning to mother, meanwhile."

Mrs. von Ratenow sat at the window, sorting a huge pile of stockings, while she drew each one over her hand, gazing sharply at it through her spectacles.

"It is sweet and dutiful in you, Elsa," she said in the course of conversation, and more gently than she usually spoke. "But see, old gentlemen have their peculiarities ; you must not think that your father does not love you because he says that he is willing for you to stay with us. It may seem harsh and unkind to you and others also ; but the reasons you must look for in his hard life, in the seclusion in which he has always insisted upon living, wholly without pleasures. Perhaps in time he will become more sociable."

Who would have recognized by these words the harsh, decided woman, who to-day tried to hold up the father's conduct in the mildest light to the child? "Greet your father for me," she called after her, as the young girl turned to go.

Frieda was evidently in the worst possible humor. She lay back in the carriage, wrapped closely in her soft fur cloak, and did not utter a word. At length she took out a dainty little purse and shook out the contents into her fine lawn handkerchief.

"It is not nearly enough, Moritz," said she then, playing with the coins. "You must pay Drewendt's bill yourself. I will have it made out to-day."

Without further remark, he drew out his pocket-book and silently handed her several bank-notes. She took them, put them into her purse with the other money, and then put it in her pocket.

"Moritz, may I buy the little étagère for my drawing-room?" she asked, gazing pleadingly at him with her blue eyes.

He turned toward her vexedly, but his irritated expression vanished when he gazed at the beautiful face which smiled at him so seductively from beneath the black fur cap.

"How fond you are of such rubbish," he said. "As you like, but we will soon be forced to hold an auction, you have so many things, eh? But how much does the thing cost?"

"Oh, not very much; a hundred marks, perhaps, Moritz."

He was silent, and Elsa did not know what to say, then the carriage stopped before the Major's house, and she got out. She crossed the bare hall, ascended the slanting stairs, stood irresolutely at the door of her father's room, and then entered the little kitchen.

Old Susan had just placed a couple of wine-glasses on a tray, and her trembling hands were trying to uncork a bottle of Rhine wine.

"Give it here, Susan," said the girl smiling; "I am stronger than you."

"Merciful heavens!" cried the old woman, joyfully. "Dear Elsa! Miss Elsa! And you have grown to be such a big girl! And I knew it would be so! We have not had a guest for ten years, and to-day they come from all directions."

Elsa placed the bottle of Rhine wine on the tray. "Call me Elsa, as you used to, Susan; but who is with papa? I do not want to disturb him."

"You must guess," cried the old woman, smiling, and tied on a fresh apron. "Now you are curious, Elsa, I see that, just as your mother was; well"—and

she came close up to the girl—"it is the Bennewitzer!
I did not recognize him at all," she continued. "Here
came a fine gentleman in black clothes, and asked for
the Major, his cousin. Had I told your papa first, he
surely would not have received him, but I did not, but
opened the door at once, and there they sat together in
a moment. Well, let them wrangle, Elsa dear, I think
it will do no harm. Do you know, until now the two
have fought like cat and dog about the inheritance.
And now—but will you not carry the wine in, Elsa?"

"Did papa call for wine?" asked the young girl.

"Oh, what are you thinking of?" replied the old
woman, shrugging her shoulders. "I only thought
that when a relative came to call one should treat him
properly."

At this moment the Major's voice rang out so loudly
and angrily that Susan, who was about to hand the
girl the tray, set it down again in alarm.

"Oh, heavens, Elsa, he is angry," she stammered,
and in fact exclamations of a man excited to the greatest fury now rang in the ear of the trembling girl.
The next moment she had hurried across the corridor,
opened a door and stood on the threshold of the room,
deathly pale, but with an expression of the utmost self-
possession.

"Papa, I trust I do not disturb you?" asked she,
advancing toward the old man, who, standing in the
middle of the room, a letter in his hand, his face deeply
flushed, stared at her as at an apparition.

The stately man who leaned carelessly against the window yonder bore not the slightest resemblance to his excited, angry cousin ; he was a gentleman in appearance from head to foot, and he seemed also to have preserved perfectly his inner calm; his face, at least, with the sad expression about the mouth, was completely unmoved.

"You do not disturb us at all, Miss von Hegebach," said he, with a bow, "in fact it is a welcome interruption. I was just trying to explain a misunderstanding on your father's part, and this was made difficult for me by new misunderstandings——"

"Papa ! " the lovely young girl had clasped the gray old man in her two arms. "Dear papa, I am so glad to be with you again," and she leaned against him as though she would protect him from all harm in this world. ·

Major von Hegebach had apparently wholly lost his presence of mind; with one hand he smoothed his daughter's hair, and with the other pushed her away.

"Afterwards, afterwards, my child—I am occupied with—with this gentleman——"

"Your daughter does not disturb us at all, cousin. I think we had better sit down and discuss the whole affair calmly, as is proper for men in the presence of a lady," said the Bennewitzer, and drew his chair up to the table covered with cigar boxes and newspapers. "Pray, William," he then continued, placing a chair for Elsa, "let us speak calmly. You know that I have

come here in no unfriendly mood, and you also know
with which of us fate has dealt most hardly."

Hegebach had seated himself, at a pleading gesture
from Elsa. For a moment there was silence in the
smoky old room.

"We two, William," the Bennewitzer began anew,
"cannot help it that our uncle, God forgive him, made
his will thus and not otherwise ; we must think no more
of that. Your claims, as you must admit to yourself,
and as your lawyer should tell you, are untenable. I
have not even the right to divide the estate and fortune
which I have inherited, and which now belong to me ;
but I have the right to make you the proposition which
I mentioned before, and I meant honestly and kindly
with you. Accept this proposition, William, if not for
your sake, for your daughter's.'

"I will not accept it," said the Major, "and await
further results."

"For Heaven's sake be prudent, William," pleaded
the Bennewitzer, glancing at the young girl.

"I know what I am doing, thank you."

With trembling hands, the old man took a package
of papers and laid them in another place, opened and
shut the cover of his cigar case with nervous haste.
Elsa looked from one to the other in perplexity.

"It is a very material matter in question, Miss von
Hegebach," the Bennewitzer turned to the young girl ;
"your father of late has believed that since stern fate
has robbed me of both sons, and thus of the heirs

of the estate, that he has claims upon it. I do not know how he has been persuaded to bring these claims into court; in any case he has been badly advised. I came to-day to prevent the beginning of this perfectly useless lawsuit, and wished——"

" To put a plaster on my mouth ! " the Major interrupted, violently. "I thank you again for your offer of assistance when I have good right to make claims."

The Bennewitzer rose. " I meant well, William ; far be it from me to urge anything upon you; enforce your claims."

He took a hat with a wide band of bombazine from the nearest chair, and offered his hand to the young girl. " I should be very happy to meet my charming cousin under pleasanter circumstances. God bless you, Miss von Hegebach ! "

The next moment the door had closed behind him.

" Papa ! " said the girl sadly, after the old man, as if wholly forgetful of her presence, had rummaged for some time in the pigeon-holes of his desk, among letters and papers. " Papa ! "

Hegebach started and rubbed his forehead.

" Papa, I should like to talk with you for a little while."

He ceased his search and stared at her.

" Papa, I merely wished to tell you that I should have come to you so gladly, and kept house for you, read to you in the evenings and arranged your room neatly." There must have been something in her

5

voice which compelled him to listen to her.   He
seated himself, and rested his head in one hand.

" And I should have been so glad to nurse you when
you are ill, papa, and you would no longer have been so
lonely for—aunt Ratenow—"   The clear, girlish voice
suddenly died away in shyness and sadness.   " Let
me stay with you, papa, I am so sorry for you," she
cried, throwing her arms around the old man's neck.
"'You are always so lonely, you cannot be happy."

" No, Elsa, that cannot be," he replied, but he did
not shake off the little hand.   " You are unfortunate,
poor child, in that you must call such a beggar as I am
father.   It could have been otherwise.   But whom
fate has once placed on a worn-out horse, will never
in all his life mount a respectable one.   I told aunt
Ratenow how much I have to live upon, twenty dollars
a month !   That sounds ridiculous, does it not ?   The
rest of my pension goes to pay old debts which my
honor obliges me to liquidate, and which will require
years before they are paid."

" Papa ! " she wished to interrupt, but he took the
words out of her mouth.

" It is best as Mrs. von Ratenow proposed to me
yesterday :   You shall undertake the education of the
little Ratenows, and receive a suitable salary for that,
and besides, be like a child of the house.   That is
more fortunate than hundreds of others in your position have, and for the rest—we will wait," he concluded.

The young girl had sprung up, and stared at the speaker's pale face. But she did not say a word. She only suddenly realized that a sweet, golden, careless girlhood no longer awaited her. As if wrapped in gray shadow, the dear old house suddenly rose before her eyes. She no longer had a right to a home, she must earn it by service rendered. She had suddenly been pushed from the position of a child into one of thankfulness. Yes, how could she have fancied that in this world love and kindness would be given without expecting a return? They had educated a governess for themselves, that was all.

An indescribably bitter feeling filled the young girl's heart ; it was not dread of work, it was the pain of a great disappointment.

"Good-by, papa," said she, putting on her hat, "I will visit you as often as "—she paused—in her bitterness she had wished to say, "as often as my mistress ——" but then she thought of Moritz's kind face, "as often as I am permitted," she corrected herself.

He gave her his hand. "Things will be better, Elsa, you are still so young."

She nodded, "Good-by, papa," then she went. How differently she had come ! She stood in the door-way with a gloomy face. The elegant carriage which had brought her just then turned the corner of the street. Moritz came for her. She must wait for him.

"How you look, Elsa," he said, as he sprang out to

•

help her into the carriage.   " Has any one vexed you,
little girl ? "   And he took her hand.

" When do you wish me to begin my instruction ? "
was the answer, as they rolled away in the carriage.
" And do you not first wish to examine my testimo-
nials ? "

He looked up.   Her voice sounded so strangely, her
lips were pressed together as if in pain.

" The instruction ? " he asked.   " Oh, yes ! mother
wished to ask you, I believe, to give the children a little
elementary instruction.   Will you, Elsa ? "

" It is all arranged," replied she.   " I was not consulted."

" Has anything occurred to wound you, Elsa ?   It
was the intention of no one, believe me," he added
gently, watching the girl's pale face.

She looked at him with eyes shining with tears. " Moritz, I will do anything, I will be with your children night and day, but offer me no money for it, I cannot bear it ! " she sobbed.

"Why Elsa, Elsa, how falsely you judge it ! " he cried, startled. And as the carriage stopped before the house door at this moment, he said, " I beg you to go upstairs to Aunt Lott, Elsa; I will only see mother for a moment and then come upstairs at once and speak with you."

Elsa had stood in her room and gazed out at the storm and rain ; she no longer wept ; she had suddenly become calm. Yesterday lay far behind her, it seemed to her that she had been dreaming. Why had she forgotten what Aunt Ratenow had told her when she was a child, " You must learn to stand on your own feet." But who thinks of the needs of life when among gay, young companions, when existence resembles a May morning ?

" Elsa ! " called a voice. She turned. Aunt Ratenow stood before her.

" I am very sorry, Elsa, that you have such a false idea of what was meant most kindly. I cannot bestow everything upon you. I must repeat to you that your circumstances are not such as to enable you to flit through life like a gay butterfly ; you must be an industrious bee. If you instruct our children, of course you will receive a salary for it, as would any other— that I can and must not spare you ; it is a false pride which makes you hesitate to accept it, and when you consider the matter you will see this. Life is long, my child. However, I will not force the hateful money into your hands, but save it for you, so that you will have a little capital. But no one compels you to undertake the children's instruction, Elsa—do you hear? You are a guest in my house and can remain one as long as you choose; the decision rests with you, Elsa."

"I accept the offer and will undertake the instruction," said the girl softly.

"That is right, Elsa. For the rest everything shall be as of old. How is your father?"

"He was excited; he had a dispute with the Bennewitzer, whom I found there."

"The Bennewitzer?" cried Mrs. von Ratenow, so loudly that the girl looked at her in alarm. "And you mention that so casually. Did he see you?"

"Yes, aunt."

"And what did he want?"

Elsa was silent for a moment. She had felt that her father was about to yield to a false idea.

"It was about Bennewitz," said she. "Father, I believe, wishes to compel a portion to be given him by the courts."

"Is he mad?" cried the old lady, crimson with anger, and then remembering that the man's daughter stood before her, she added, "You do not understand, Elsa, and I do not mean unkindly. I must speak to your father; he will stir up a fine commotion. What does he look like, the Bennewitzer, Elsa?" And she patted the girl's face. "We will be very comfortable here this winter," she added, without awaiting an answer.

"Aunt Lott," said the girl, with a sad smile, as later she entered her cosey room, "if I shall ever again forget it, pray remind me."

"Of what, my little rosebud?"

"That I am a poor girl."

VI.

But yet she could not always think of it. Elsa had
wandered through the garden the next morning, and
every tree had nodded to her: "Do you remember
me?" Every spot where as a child she had played,
had whispered sweet, confidential words to her young,
pained heart; the sun had shone so brightly and
warmly over the stately old house, and in all the
country round she knew every roof, every wind-mill,
every hill. No; she was at home, therefore she was
not poor.

How could she be sad in the midst of such gayety,
happiness and coseyness? It was so pleasant in the
comfortable dining-room at the well-spread table, so
pleasant when Aunt Ratenow told stories of the past;
it was like a sunbeam when Mrs. Frieda laughed and
the children joined in so clearly, while Moritz sat at
the head of the table, carving the roast and providing
for every one.

"Elsa, are you really no longer hungry? Pray eat
more, little girl; see this appetizing bit of lamb, eh?
That is right, taste it." And after dinner he took the

little boy on his back, and then there was a wild romp out in the garden, up and down the paths, all together. What laughter and noise there was, until Frieda declared, " Pray stop, Moritz, we cannot catch you ! "

And then the walks out into the country those lovely autumn days, with Frieda and Aunt Ratenow. Sometimes the young lady's elegant coupé rolled through the streets of the little city, and the shop-keepers rushed out to open the carriage-door and assist the ladies to alight. And in the evening there were always guests ; and then John knocked at Aunt Lott's door to ask if Miss von Hegebach would not come down to the young mistress. And how quickly the little hands could arrange the wavy hair and fasten on the pink sash, especially when the old man added, " They are to have some music."

Who would have thought that the hated piano and singing lessons could have such happy results ? And who would have thought that anything in this world could sing and mourn like that little brown violin which Lieutenant Bernardi held in his arms ?

The beginning of Elsa's activity had been postponed. She did not know that Moritz had privately told his wife, " Listen, Frieda dear, you absolutely do not wish the children to be bothered with lessons before the beginning of January ? " And when Elsa asked the young mother to fix a time for the beginning of lessons she had replied very calmly, " We have plenty of time to decide that ; I cannot think of shutting up the chil-

dren before the middle of January. Besides, Moritz
must first fit up a school-room with comfortable seats ;
the eldest child is growing so fast and beyond her
strength, and besides—the children could do nothing
before Christmas."

It was useless for Aunt Ratenow to talk, for Frieda's
wishes, as their mother, must be respected, and besides
it was far too pleasant for young Mrs. von Ratenow
to have a companion during the quiet time of morning
for her to listen to "sensible advice." - And Moritz?
Oh, he was henpecked, as the old lady told Aunt
Lott confidentially, within her own four walls.

Elsa had met her former school-mate, Miss Annie
Cramm, in Frieda's charming drawing-room with its
blue hangings. She had returned to her father's house
immediately after her confirmation, and had been out in
society for two years. Her thin face was as pale and
immature as ever, her blue eyes as light, and her hair
even more straw-colored, but it was arranged with the
utmost care, and the handsome gowns fitted the young
lady's somewhat angular figure faultlessly.

"She is a goose," said Frieda very frankly.

"But with golden feathers, dear child," added Aunt
Ratenow ; "that excuses much."

Elsa chatted with Annie Cramm to her heart's content of boarding-school days ; the young lady even
sometimes came to see Aunt Lott. She could sigh
deeply and look very mournful, and she kept a journal
in which she conscientiously recorded every ball and

the name of every one with whom she danced a quadrille or cotillon. As she possessed a thin soprano voice, she was often present at Frieda's musical evenings. She preferred to sing alone, and always appeared in the most faultless costumes, although not always adapted to the situation and person, thus not seldom exciting the young hostess's mockery, the latter being morbidly sensitive to all that was not *chic*.

Elsa's black cashmere gown was condemned once for all, in her opinion, as "frightfully respectable." But what could Frieda do? At first she had intended replenishing the girl's more than simple wardrobe from her own store, but this had been energetically opposed by her husband, usually so bidable.

"If Elsa needs anything," he declared, "mother will attend to it for her as she has always done before. Besides, what could she do with your cast-off wardrobe? She is a head taller than you. I positively will not consent that she shall wear your old clothes, Frieda! Why stamp her with poverty in the sight of every one?"

And so the slender blonde girl always appeared in her simple black gown, which doubly increased her peculiar loveliness.

Things had now gone so far that twice in the week, on certain days, lights were placed on the piano, and there was music from four o'clock in the afternoon until midnight.

"I can do nothing but blow on a comb," declared

Moritz one afternoon when Elsa met him coming down-
stairs with a pile of music under his arm, "and if
necessity demands whistle *'Heil dir in. Siegeskranz!'*
I appear at supper punctually, and if afterwards a few
songs are sung I enjoy listening. But I know nothing
of your symphonies. Good-by, Elsa ; and keep a
couple of songs for me."

And as he had nothing to do outside, he went up to
his mother's room, lit a cigar, and seated himself comfortably in his late father's arm-chair. Mother and son
were never at a loss for conversation ; the household
and estate would in themselves furnish topics, and they
always discussed everything together. The practical
old lady was ever ready with good advice, and so they
were very soon engaged in an agricultural discussion.
Then they came to city news, and finally Moritz told
her that he had spoken with the Bennewitzer a few
days before in Magdeburg, and the latter had told him
that his cousin had really brought suit against him.

" The fool will have to wound his head before he
realizes that there are walls," said Mrs. von Ratenow.
" I have lamed my tongue talking, and half paralyzed
my hand writing, but he clings to his fancied 'good
rights' with a firmness worthy of a better cause."

She was silent, but the knitting-needles clicked more
energetically than ever. Nothing made the old lady
more irritable than when any one refused to be taught
by her.

" Say, my boy," she asked suddenly, " is it really only

the desire for music which brings the black **Lieutenant** here so often with his violin ?"

"Probably," replied Moritz. "They do nothing else but make music, and forget to eat and drink."

"But do you know, Moritz? I place no dependence upon you, in such things you are a child. I must investigate for myself."

"Oh, mother, **Aunt** Lott **sits** there—knits and is delighted——"

"Yes, she **is** the right one," nodded **Mrs.** von Ratenow, still between jest and earnest, "a good soul, but in spite **of her age she would be** the **first one to fall in love** with Bernardi."

Moritz laughed loudly.

"It is really no laughing **matter, my boy ; you also** fell deeply **in love once,** do **you know? And others** have eyes in their heads and fresh young blood in their veins," **and** with these words she took off her neat tulle cap, and smoothing her shining and still brown hair, **she added,** "Give me the cap with the lilac ribbons, from my **top drawer, Moritz.** So, that is it; I thank you, and now **we too will revel in music for once.**"

The large **man had closed the drawer again, and** brushed some ashes from his dark-blue clothes. "**Well,** mother dear, if you mean Elsa——"

"I mean nothing at all, Moritz. Will you come with me ?"

"Willingly, so that you may see that no love potions are being brewed, you all too anxious little mother."

Down in the drawing-room the chandeliers and lamps were already lighted ; they had just finished a Kreutzer concerto, and were animatedly discussing it when mother and son entered. Frieda sat at the piano practicing a difficult passage, Lieutenant Bernardi had put down his violin and stood beside Elsa, who was looking over some music. Annie Cramm and Aunt Lott sat near the window, their cheeks flushed deeply with interest.

"We should like to hear a few songs," said Moritz, in excuse of their sudden appearance, and with a sonorous "Good evening, ladies, good evening, dear Bernardi," Aunt Ratenow seated herself in the corner beside Aunt Lott. Moritz smiled to himself; she was no diplomat, his magnificent old mother, she always went straight to the point. It amused him greatly to watch her.

Miss Annie Cramm was urged to sing. Elsa sat quietly in the deep window recess, and her sweet, childish face peeped out from behind the heavy blue curtains which formed a fine background for the blonde head. Bernardi had gone to the opposite end of the room ; he leaned against Frieda's book-case directly opposite Elsa.

"A very handsome fellow," Mrs. von Ratenow admitted to herself, "so slender and aristocratic-looking, and with the best of manners ; no wonder if——"

Then Annie Cramm's high voice began, a voice which had such an alarming effect upon the high-shouldered, thin figure of the singer.

"Very beautiful, my dear young lady," said the old lady in praise, "but I do not understand it, it is too high-flown for me."

"Mamma dear, what a crime! It was by Wagner," cried Frieda.

"I do not know him," was the response, given with unshaken calm.

"Yes, you see that is because you will never go to the opera with us, mamma, when we are in Berlin," complained the younger lady.

"Child, I am really somewhat proud of my nerves, but I always tell myself the present music is beyond me. I tremble in all my limbs after the first act, and have but one thought—will they never stop?—You who are always talking about your nerves can yet endure such things for hours. Elsa, will you not sing us a simple song?"

The young girl went to the piano with crimson cheeks.

"We can try the old song with the new setting," proposed Frieda; she secretly was in a quiver of horror at her mother-in-law's views, and there were several discords in the first few bars of the introduction. But now a sweet full alto voice began:

> "Ah, who in this world is like me left to pine?
> No father, no mother, no fortune is mine.
> And nothing else have I to claim or to keep,
> Save only two brown eyes with which I may weep.

" Far over the fields howls the wild autumn wind.
My lover was faithless to me and unkind,
Because on my bosom no jewels bright shone.
Ah, has ever such longing as mine yet been known?

" Down there flows the river, so black and so deep.
Ah, could I but lie there forever asleep !
Three flowers, three rosebuds, a shroud white as snow ;
There would I rest sweetly, nor know pain or woe."

"Bravo, Elsa ! " said the old lady, holding out her
hand to the girl. The others were silent. Bernardi
raised his violin and began to play the simple mournful
melody, and then a wild strain, a chaos of tones through

which the melody could be heard, and finally the grief-stricken cry of the last stanza.

The two young people gazed at each other while he played, then the girl's moist brown eyes were lowered, and the flush on her cheeks gave place to pallor. Silently she seated herself near Aunt Lott. Bernardi had put down the violin and received warm praise; only Aunt Ratenow was silent.

"It is an old song," said she at length, "with an ever new melody. Do you not say so, Frieda? Elsa!" she then cried, as they went to the dining-room, and the young girl was about to take the chair next the officer's, "Elsa dear, let Moritz or Aunt Lott sit there, and help me a little here; I have gout in my arm again."

Elsa was ready at once, but Moritz stared at his mother, this feminine strategy fairly terrified him. And all so unnecessary, as he thought. There he sat, the dangerous man, and chatted on common-place topics with his pale neighbor, peeled an orange for Frieda, and told regimental stories. Conversation was carried on briskly around the table; finally Moritz began to talk of old regimental days, and the men became quite excited.

It was late when they rose from table; the carriage had long been waiting for Annie Cramm, outside in the wind and rain. Now she wrapped herself in her velvet cloak and took leave in the hall.

"Lieutenant, may I offer you a seat in my carriage?" she asked.

6

He stood beside Elsa, his cap under his arm, talking to her. The large room was but dimly lighted ; still Annie saw that he drew the girl's slender, half-resisting hand to his lips.

"Will you drive with me, Lieutenant?" she asked again impatiently ; "it is already very late, and I am in a hurry."

"Thank you, Miss Cramm, but I prefer to walk, the exercise will do me good," he replied, with his courtliest bow.

Annie Cramm drew the veil over her pale face and forgot to bid Elsa Hegebach good-by ; Moritz escorted her to her carriage, and then shook the hand of the young officer who was just descending the steps. He stood there for a while gazing after Bernardi, looked up at the sky, and finally his eyes remained fixed upon two windows of the upper story, behind which a light was just then visible.

He began to whistle a few bars from "Boccaccio" and went into the house. "Frieda," he said to his beautiful little wife, who was closing the piano in the drawing-room, "is there anything in the air?"

"Now you have made another discovery, Moritz," she replied, laughing.

"Yes, Bernardi and—— "

"Oh, nonsense ! she is too coarse," she interrupted him.

"No, no ! I mean Elsa."

"Good heavens !" was the instant reply, "if that is

all you know—that is simply impossible—he does not think of such a thing."

"But if she, Elsa——"

"Well, if she does! I had two lovers before you, Moritz, and I am still alive."

He did not hear the last, the words had suddenly occurred to him which the girl had sung earlier in the evening :

"Far over the fields howls the wild autumn wind.
My lover was faithless to me and unkind."

"It would be a shame," said he, and drew his hand over his eyes.

But upstairs a girl sat on the deepest window seat, and held her hands clasped over her beating heart. She was not poor, she was so rich that she would not have changed with any one in the world. How was it possible that life could be so beautiful? Was it possible that any one could love her, love her as his eyes plainly said? And she sat there for a long while, staring at the lights of the city, until one after the other was extinguished. Aunt Lott's calm breathing could be heard in the next room, she slept so sweetly and soundly, and forgot to rise and say to her who had forgotten it all this time, "Child, what are you dreaming of? You are only a poor girl!"

VII.

IT was winter. At Christmas the snow had lain
white and shining over the quiet country and the roofs
of the houses. It had snowed until New Year's day.
The streets and roads were as hard and smooth as the
best parquet, and Moritz had had the horses rough
shod, for there was to be a sleigh-ride, a large sleighing
party.

Young Mrs. von Ratenow, in a dark-blue velvet
costume edged with fur, was just drawing on her gloves
before the large mirror in her bedroom. Moritz declared that she looked sweet enough to kiss, and he
would have looked forward to the whole affair if only
this unfortunate Bernardi were not to drive Elsa.

The young wife shrugged her dainty shoulders
scarcely perceptibly. "This eternal anxiety about
Elsa! Mamma speaks of nothing else, and so do you.
Is she then anything so very much better than other
girls?"

"Yes!" replied Moritz warmly. "She has a warm,
loving heart, and when she feels anything she does so
deeply and with all her heart. Superficial trifling or
even coquetry is wholly foreign to the little girl."

"You seem to have studied this girlish heart very accurately," was the apparently calm reply; but Moritz knew the accent of this complaisant tone only too well not to be sure that the speaker was very irritated.

"Frieda, I beg you—I have known her ever since she was born, as I know our children!" His honest eyes gazed fairly in alarm at her face which was so blooming beneath the feathers of her hat. But she calmly fastened the last button of her long gloves, and picked up her coquettish little muff. "I believe the gentlemen are already in the drawing-room." Then she floated past him without paying the slightest attention to the man's hand which was held out to her conciliatingly.

It was not the first time that the young wife had spoken thus; in her opinion the way people troubled themselves about this girl was horrible, for she really had quite an easy time in the world. Who would lift a hand for her were she at home with her surly old father? And mamma Ratenow was always emphasizing the remark that she wished to prevent a misfortune, and Moritz, as faithful echo, joined in. That became tiresome after a while. What did it matter if an officer did pay attentions to her? She amused herself, one could not grudge her that, there was really no danger, for—he was far too prudent, Bernardi, and Elsa! absurd!

Her cheeks still wore the flush of displeasure as she entered the drawing-room and greeted Captain von Franken and Lieutenant Bernardi, the two gentlemen who were to have the honor of driving the ladies.

The Captain, a slender, handsome man and great admirer of young Mrs. von Ratenow, jestingly sank on one knee, and handed his lady a bouquet of pale yellow roses.

Elsa held a bouquet of violets ; her face was radiant.

" Oh, Frieda, see ! Snow and ice and these lovely flowers ; it is like a dream ! "

Like a dream, like a sweet dream was life. The sun shone so brightly upon the sunny landscape, the air was so clear and cold, so delightfully pure, the sleigh-bells rang, and the line of sleighs flew over the road ; how beautiful the world is when the heart is full of happiness ! The young girl's face had but once saddened, that was when she passed the house where her father lived. She looked up ; he stood at the window, in dressing-gown and cap, but he did not return the girl's eager nod and greeting.

Papa was always so absorbed in thought. Decidedly, at times papa did not know that he possessed a daughter.

But then the band began to play, and they talked—of nothing at all and yet so much. " My Christian name is Bernard," he had told her, and carefully drawn the warm lap-robe over her.

" Bernard Bernardi, that sounds very pretty," said Elsa.

" Your cousin is a true Providence to us," he went on. " Only fancy, where are we to dance this evening but in the hall at the castle ? Really charming people ! "

"Where is Annie Cramm? Who is driving her?" asked Elsa.

He laughed so that his white teeth shone under his black moustache.

"Ensign Hubart was ordered to that post."

"Oh, how horrible! Annie is so good."

"Good? Is that all? That is very little."

"That is a great deal, sir," said the young girl, her brown, childish eyes gazing at him very seriously.

He must look at her continually; he knew every feature of this pure, fresh face, and it was delightful to drive beside this lovely girl who was so different from the others, so—so—he did not know the right word himself—so true-hearted, so lovable, so truly womanly. And while he gazed fixedly at her he thought of his home, his mother; and then he suddenly stood in the old-fashioned sitting-room, and beside him—stood Elsa.

"There drive hunger and thirst together," remarked the fat Referendar Golling to Lieutenant von Rost, and puffed the smoke of his cigar out into the cold, wintry air comfortably. They were in the sleigh behind Elsa and Bernardi; neither had a lady with him, probably they did not desire one. Lieutenant von Rost here took the part of lady; he had tied a handkerchief around his arm and managed a huge crimson fan with great skill.

"Ah, well! a sleighing party is quite endurable; the good sideboards in the castle are a consoling background," yawned the Lieutenant.

"Good heavens, the man will never be so mad as to have serious intentions?" asked the Referendar.

"Oh, what do I know about it?" the officer yawned again; "it is his affair. He knows as well as the rest of us that the old lady has nothing to leave."

"He makes it a trifle hard, dear Rost, and — besides he is a good - hearted fellow."

"Yes; who is not? But this is where his good-heartedness ends," declared the Lieutenant, and dropped the eye-glass with which he had been watching the pair ahead of him.

Moritz was in the last sleigh with a pretty young

woman. He was irritable, and continually looking for Frieda and Elsa.

"Miss von Hegebach is quite far ahead, Mr. von Ratenow, Bernardi is driving her. He is at your house a great deal, is he not? His sister is a friend of mine; the father was a physician here formerly. He has quite a large practice now in B——, I believe, but nothing more. The large family—you know, Mr. von Ratenow——"

"I know his family affairs quite well," replied Moritz, crossly. He understood very well what hint was intended to be conveyed to him.

"Oh, indeed! Pardon me, dear Mr. von Ratenow," said the young woman, and stared at him. Well, then, they of the castle knew that he was not at all a good match.

Meanwhile the castle was a perfect pandemonium, as old Mrs. von Ratenow angrily told Aunt Lott. The table was set in the dining-room, and the gardener dragged half the contents of the conservatory into the hall where they were to dance. Frieda had left off mourning on January 1st punctually; to-day she gave her first large entertainment, and that an impromptu one. She had come home from a party the night before with this idea, and had set all hands and feet in the house in motion early this morning.

"Only leave me in peace," Mrs. von Ratenow told her daughter-in-law; "send me the children so that they will not be in your way, that is all that I will have to do with the affair."

In Frieda's dressing-room the elegant, pale-blue silk gown lay ready for the evening, with every article needed for her toilet.

Upstairs in Elsa's room two old hands had laid out the simple white batiste gown which had been a Christmas present to the young girl ; and the two little gilt slippers, small as those of a child, stood on the table before the old lady. Here and there she had fastened a knot of ribbon with true delight, for it was no trifle to dress her child for the first time for a dance. She had then donned her gray silk, had lighted the lamps, and chosen a romance by Hackländer. Now she waited for Elsa to assist her that she might make a quick toilet.

Gradually it grew quieter down-stairs ; the preparations were completed, it was the quiet before the storm. And now the sleigh-bells were heard outside ; there they were, Moritz, Frieda, Elsa, and all the rest.

In a few moments the light steps of the young girl came down the corridor, the door was opened, and she stood on the threshold, flushed and out of breath.

"Good evening, my dear little auntie!" she cried, and threw both arms around the old lady's neck. A breath of fresh, cold, snowy air entered the room with her.

"Was it nice, Mouse? Did you enjoy yourself? Come, drink your tea."

But the young girl hastily declined, quickly ran into her bedroom, and there she stood in the darkness for a long time, forgetting to remove coat and hat.

Aunt Lott came to help her.

"But Elsa, there you stand, and it is high time to change your dress." She fetched a light and took the child's wraps off. "Why, what is the matter, Elsa? You surely are not crying?"

The girl was silent and began to change her dress, but to-day she did not seem able to arrange her hair; the trembling hands three times tried to fasten the heavy braids, and the rose would not be adjusted.

"That is good, that is very pretty," said Aunt Lott. "You usually are not so vain."

Yes, usually, Aunt Lott. She had no suspicion for whom the child adorned herself.

At length she was ready.

"Aunt Lott, I feel so strangely to-day." She really trembled nervously.

"Why, what is the matter, child? Have you taken cold on the drive?"

"No, no. Come, aunt."

"Will you not take a few drops of cologne, Elsa?"

She did not answer; she stood motionless, and her eyes stared into space with a strangely radiant expression. She thought she heard her name again, "Elsa," and then a few simple words: "Happiness! What is happiness if not this moment?"

His voice shook so strangely as he said that. He had spoken to her of his parents on the homeward drive, how sweet and lovely his mother was, how she loved to hear him play on his violin. His father had

once played that instrument; he remembered very well
how he, when a little boy, had sat in the twilight, on his
mother's lap listening intently while his father walked
up and down the room playing. Sometimes he would
let his bow fall and come over to kiss mother and
child. Oh, yes, the little violin had witnessed much
happiness, that was why it sang so sweetly. Ah, happiness ! What is happiness if not this moment ?

And their hands suddenly clasped each other, and
Elsa shed tears, but they were tears of joy, for the
young heart rejoiced, and above them the starry heaven
arched itself.

"Elsa, come, I beg you ! " pleaded Aunt Lott.   " I
think we are the last."

She followed the gray silk train as though in a dream ;
she dreaded seeing him in the bright light, and yet her
heart beat rapidly.

There was a hum of voices in the brilliantly-lighted
hall and the adjoining dancing-room, card-tables were
arranged in Moritz's room, and Mrs. von Ratenow held
some cards in her hand. She was talking to an old
gentleman when Elsa approached her to kiss her hand.
The old lady stared at her in surprise for a moment,
the girl was so beautiful this evening; she patted her
cheek almost shyly and followed her with her eyes as
she threaded her way through the gay crowd, her head
slightly bowed, and yet so proud, the beautiful figure in
the plain white gown, through which her neck and arms
shone rosily. She paused beside Annie Cramm. This

young lady looked very cross and snappish under her wreath of white lilies ; in her lilac gown, with its over-abundant garniture of lace and flowers, she resembled a wax-figure exhibiting a new costume in the show window of a dressmaking establishment. Everything about her toilet was so elegant, from the pale lilac satin shoes to the expensive point-lace fan and the diamond butterfly which shone so dazzlingly and pretentiously on the young lady's bony neck.

"What a caricature the present fashion is," murmured Mrs. von Ratenow. "I am surprised that Annie Cramm can dance, she is so tightly laced, and how she looks!"

The first notes of the waltz rang through the room ; as if electrified the couples began to dance; it was a beautiful picture in the handsome frame.

"Where is Elsa, Lott? I do not see her," asked Mrs. von Ratenow.

"There, there!" cried the old lady. "Ratenow, the child does not dance, she flies!" she cried, in an ecstasy, and took her *lorgnon* to follow her darling with rapturous eyes.

"She still finds pleasure in it, my dear madam," remarked an old man with gold spectacles. "Good heavens, eighteen years old!"

"Tell me, my dear Councillor," asked Mrs. von Ratenow, "are you not the Bennewitzer Hegebach's adviser?"

"I have that honor, madam."

" Well——"

" Well, the Major's suit was defeated, naturally."

"Of course," nodded Mrs. von Ratenow. " Does he know it yet ? "

" He will have learned of it to-day, madam. I too am curious as to the effect it will have upon him."

Mrs. von Ratenow suddenly looked anxiously in the speaker's face. " Do you believe that he will learn a lesson from it ? "

"Oh, no indeed," replied he. " As long as the old hot head has breath, he will quarrel."

The dance was at an end, the guests withdrew to the adjoining room, to the charming little nooks among the shrubbery, or to the conservatory. Bernardi had led Elsa to Frieda's little boudoir; the girl was looking for the mistress of this apartment, in order that she might offer some assistance in her duties as hostess. No one was there but the two little girls, who, in their very short white frocks, were seated on a lounge, absorbed in one of mamma's beautiful books. Frieda's large dog sat beside them with a knowing air.

Elsa seated herself in a low arm-chair near the children and began to talk to them. The eldest laid the book on her knee. It was a charming picture, and she felt that his eyes rested upon her in admiration. She looked up and their eyes met, until, blushing deeply, she lowered her lashes again.

" Now we will soon begin to study," said the young girl, stroking the eldest girl's hair.

" I can read now, Aunt Elsa, listen ! " And, pointing out the letters with her little finger, the child read what was printed beneath the picture :

> " Love conquers all things.
> You lie ! said the penny."

Elsa looked at the picture ; it was an illustration of "Old German wit and wisdom." A bridal procession ascended the steps of a church, the young nobleman led the magnificently dressed bride, a whole crowd of stately relatives followed. Aside from them stood a poorly clad girl, with no ornaments save two long blonde braids. She had turned her back to the procession, buried her face in her apron and wept. Bernardi looked over Elsa's shoulder at the page.

The little girl asked whether the picture pleased him. He did not answer.

" Bernardi, oh—a word," suddenly said Lieutenant von Rost's voice, close behind him. He left the room with his comrade.

" What do you want, Rost ? " he asked in the next room.

" Bernardi," said the officer, removing his eye-glass, " you and I have always been frank with each other. I am frank with you now. Get leave for a while or have yourself transferred, or as far as I am concerned marry Annie Cramm——"

Bernardi grew white to the lips. " You must be plainer, Rost."

" Plainer ? Very well ; you have debts, *mon ami*,

although no enormous ones; you have neither a wealthy
uncle nor aunt, and your father possesses all possible
virtues but no earthly goods.   Still plainer?" he asked.
" You certainly seem slow of comprehension, or else you
would long ago have guessed from Ratenow's highly
constrained manner to you, the general opinion which

prevails in this hospitable house concerning your behavior.   I do not, to be sure, know how far you have
gone, and whether you still can withdraw ; in case this
is no longer possible, you may be sure of my sympathy."

Without another word, he left his comrade and returned to Elsa, who was still listening to the children's

chat. The book she had laid on a table, and was again absorbed in her happy thoughts.

" I have the honor of this dance, Miss von Hegebach," said the young officer, and with a jesting remark he led her back to the hall.

Bernardi was in the most painful frame of mind ; he forced his way through the next rooms with a gloomy face, and remained standing in the door of the hall, beside Moritz. In fact the man, usually so affable, was remarkably cool to him. Then it had gone so far that the very sparrows chatted of it on the roofs. Stroking his moustache, he went over the whole list of his relatives. Rost was right, he had not a single wealthy uncle or aunt from whom he might hope to inherit.

" Oho, Colonel ! " he heard Mrs. von Ratenow say suddenly, close behind him, " that is a matter of opinion." It was spoken so loudly and sternly.

He turned and looked into the adjoining room. The old lady in her heavy silk gown sat opposite the regimental commander at the nearest whist table; they were playing cards, and her face wore the severe expression which was peculiar to it when she prepared to defend one of her opinions.

" That is a matter of opinion," she repeated. " It is not my view. I have seen too much misery from this so-called sense of honor. I will give you an example at once."

She had finished her hand of cards, and laid her folded hands upon the table. It suddenly seemed to

7

Bernardi that she now spoke so loudly because she had
just discovered him at the door. Involuntarily he
listened.

" She was my friend, Colonel ; you surely know Major
von Welsleben and his wife ?   Well, they met and fell
in love with each other when they were mere children.
At that age one does not consider the prose of life, you
were about to say, Colonel ?   Very well, then some one
should tell the young people that it is their bounden
duty to awake from their moonlight idyll of ' love in a
cottage,' should look about in real life, and recognize
that one does not live on love and the perfume of roses.

·" Well, they were betrothed; it was an endless engagement, he an irritable man, she a nervous girl, until the
clergyman at length consecrated their unhappy marriage.
Now listen to what is coming, Colonel.   You declared
that his sense of honor would have forced him to
engage himself to the girl since he had so openly showed
her that he loved her !   A false sense of honor, sir !
My old butler, who has lived in my house for thirty-two
years—he is not one of the cleverest of men—one evening said to me, as he was setting the table, ' Mrs. von
Hegebach, this table-cloth absolutely cannot be used ; if
I draw it over this end it does not cover the other, if I
cover that end the table shows at this end.   I have tormented myself for a good hour with the thing.'   Thus it
was with the Welslebens, their whole life they spent in
drawing the table-cloth here and there, but it never was
large enough.   Children came, money grew more and

more scarce, bills poured in upon them from every
direction, joy had long since been unknown in the
house, and when the bell rang, the wife started anxiously
because she thought it must again be one of those
often presented, and alas, never paid bills. The wife
worried herself thin and sickly, and he went oftener
than was good for him to the tavern. Now, I ask you,
sir, where——"

Bernardi did not hear the rest. Suddenly he went
up to Frieda and begged for an extra dance. She
declined. "My dear Bernardi, take pity on Miss
Cramm." He bowed and left the room.

Elsa's brown eyes sought some one. Lieutenant
Rost knew very well whom. He was very sorry for
the girl, as sorry as he could be for any one. He would
gladly have settled a few thousand dollars upon Bernardi, so that these little feet might trip beside him
through life. "On my honor, she is charming!"

Meanwhile, Bernardi had paced up and down the
broad garden path in stormy haste. "If you still can
withdraw"—the words rang in his ears. He grew dizzy.
It seemed to him that he could murder the man who
had spoken these words. But they were all right, and
that was the devilish part of it! Could he withdraw
now without a scandal? He had exchanged no definite
words with her—in an hour perhaps he would have.
And yet she must have read in his eyes a thousand
times, as he had in her clear brown, childish eyes, that
they loved each other dearly.

But what foolishness! The old lady's description was so hopelessly horrible, so fearfully true; a miserable prospect! He pushed the hair back from his forehead; a melody suddenly came to his mind, simple words :

> "Far over the fields howls the wild autumn wind.
> My lover was faithless to me and unkind."

And again he saw the picture which he had seen shortly before, and the weeping girl took the form of Elsa von Hegebach.

No, he could not, he would not withdraw; he could not live if Elsa von Hegebach were to look upon him as a despicable, faithless man. He had held her hand in his for one rapturous moment, and love was too holy, woman too sacred to him. There must be an outlet from his difficulty, at worst he could resign. Suddenly he returned with great strides to the house, and through the drawing-room to the card-room.

"My dear Mrs. von Ratenow," said he with a deep bow, "may I ask you for a short interview?" He spoke softly, and gazed calmly at the intelligent face which was turned to him in astonishment.

She did not answer immediately, but she put down the cards. "Go to my sitting-room. I will follow you," she replied as softly. It was well that the others were talking so loudly, and that just then the music began again.

Mrs. von Ratenow looked after him as he disappeared

behind the portières. "Here we have it," she said to herself. "My dear Councillor, will you take my hand for fifteen minutes or so? Thank you." And passing through the ball-room, she followed the young officer to her room. It was lighted by but a single lamp, and from the twilight a grave, pale face met her gaze.

"Well, dear Bernardi?"

"My dear Mrs. Ratenow, a short time ago you pronounced a severe sentence upon—that—" he hesitated.

"I know what you mean," said she. "You surely do not wish to force me to retract my remark?" It sounded jokingly, but her eyes were grave, almost stern.

"Do you not think an exception possible?" he asked.

"No!" she replied shortly, and seated herself in the nearest chair.

"Not even when a firm, honest purpose is united to a heart full of true love?"

He spoke with deep emotion; the old lady looked up at him—almost compassionately.

"Good heavens! They all think that; they all believe that, but it is the vain delusion of a lover, Bernardi."

"I would resign, dear madam. It is true that our rank demands great outward show; the lot of a poor officer is most miserable. I would never offer it to Elsa von Hegebach—I——"

"Elsa von Hegebach?" Mrs. von Ratenow rose and approached the young man in her rustling silk gown. "If you mean Elsa von Hegebach, I tell you she is a poor girl, and would never allow a man to give up his career for her sake only to lead a discontented, empty life with her. She is far too sensible for that, sir ; and I am firmly convinced that you are honorable enough not to make such a proposition to a child who does not yet know what it means to bind herself forever. Up to this time she has never known the needs of life."

She had spoken loudly and violently, and now continued, " Do you think that when you have left off the gay coat you can live like a day-laborer ? The world of to-day ruins one for that from his very youth. Go, Bernardi, I should never have thought you so foolish."

" I love Miss von Hegebach," he replied, and gazed firmly into her excited face.

" Yes, indeed, you have plunged in over your ears ! I saw it coming, unfortunately."

" And I am loved in return."

" Ah ! " The old lady tossed back her cap-strings impatiently. " What does such a child know of love ? Do not talk to me of that, Bernardi ; at that age one has no judgment, and even if——"

" And even if—" he repeated ; " dear Mrs. von Rate-now, and even if—— ? "

" Well, she will forget you, Bernardi !—Oh, no, no," she continued, " do not be foolish ! I believe that you are in love with the girl, she is a pretty little thing, but —you will not die of it. I must beg you in all serious-ness, my dear Lieutenant Bernardi, to look upon this conversation as ended. It is an impossibility, and neither your parents nor Elsa's father, neither I nor my son could be pleased. I cannot speak prettily to you of great honor and so on ; you know I consider you a charming man, Bernardi, and a man of honor; do not make the child unhappy ! I mean well with you and with her."

" I am breaking no promise to Miss von Hegebach ; far be it from me to make her unhappy. Accept my thanks, madam."

He bowed formally and turned toward the door.

" Wait, Bernardi, I cannot let you go thus ! " cried Mrs. von Ratenow; and her diamonds sparkled like coals of fire as she turned quickly. " First promise that you will see the child no more."

" I will leave the city as soon as possible, madam."

" Thank you, dear Bernardi."

And as the door closed behind him she stood for some time on the same spot, her head bowed. Then she drew her hand across her forehead, as though to banish an unpleasant thought.

" Pardon, gentlemen," she said, a few minutes later, in the card-room, " I am again at your disposal. Eh, are we winners, Councillor ? "

And evening deepened into night, they had danced together once more. He had been very gay, Lieutenant Bernardi, thought the young ladies ; the gentlemen declared that he had taken more champagne than was necessary. He had pocketed a bow of ribbon which floated to his feet as Elsa danced past; he had pressed the girl's trembling hand once more, and then he had left with his courtliest bow, without once looking into the moist longing eyes, and outside on the street he had taken Lieutenant von Rost's arm.

" Why, you are not going home already ? " he declared coldly. And then all the bachelors had repaired to their club.

" Hey, what is the matter ? " Dolling asked Lieutenant von Rost, and pointed to Bernardi, who was talking loudly to an older comrade, as though to drown an inner voice.

" Oh," replied Von Rost, " he is at the crisis, he will get over it soon."

" Ah, auntie, do not go to sleep yet," begged Elsa. She had put on a wrapper, and sat on the edge of the old lady's bed.

"My darling, open your heart to me," said the sentimental old lady with the childlike nature.

" I love him so dearly ! " whispered the fresh girlish lips. Then she said nothing more, the two only silently pressed each other's hands.

VIII.

THE day after such an entertainment is the same in every house : the ladies look tired out, the gentlemen have headaches, the rooms are still disordered, the servants sleepy—but worst of all is breakfast.

It was almost twelve o'clock when the household assembled in the dining-room for this meal. Mrs. Ratenow was sternly critical, and evidently not in the best temper. Frieda yawned frequently, and Aunt Lott revelled in recollections of the preceding evening, and once more described each toilet accurately.

"Where is Elsa ?" Moritz asked at length. He had sat there silently, eating and drinking up to this time.

"She is coming immediately," said Aunt Lott. "She was not quite ready; she wishes to go to her father, he is not well."

"I believe it," said old Mrs. von Ratenow.

"Did not the child look charming, cousin ?" asked Aunt Lott.

"Oh, yes," was the cool reply. "But when are the lessons to begin ?"

"Not for the present," declared Moritz calmly. "I intend postponing them until Easter. And I wished to propose to you, Aunt Lott, that you change your plan this year, and pass your prescribed eight weeks in Z—— now, and take Elsa with you."

Aunt Lott's good old face suddenly grew deathly pale. "Go away now?" she stammered, "when Elsa is so happy—pray, Moritz——"

"That does not suit me at all," declared Frieda; "I prefer that the children should at least learn to sit still."

"Oh, yes, Frieda!" cried Aunt Lott, more tragically than ever. "Offer any reason. If the child goes away now, a happiness will be murdered!"

The young wife laughed merrily. "Aunt, you deserve, while still alive, to have a monument erected to you under a weeping willow surrounded by roses."

"I should be very sorry, cousin," cried Mrs. von Ratenow, raising her voice, "were you to assist an affair which we are using all our efforts to prevent."

The old lady's face had paled visibly. "I have not assisted, dear Ratenow," said she gravely and decidedly. "In such an affair no one can; it is a wonder sent by God. It comes——"

"It comes," Frieda interrupted her, still laughing—

"It comes like perfume on the breeze;
It comes as softly as at night.
From darkest clouds shines the moon's calm light!"

"Oh, yes, to be sure," said Mrs. von Ratenow, "that

is very pretty to write in an album, but this is something different. Do not excite yourself, she will be sensible."

" How many girls' lives have been ruined by these words," murmured Aunt Lott.

" This is really no laughing matter, Frieda." The old lady's eyes rested reproachfully on the laughing, beautiful face of her daughter-in-law.

The young lady was about to open her mouth to reply, when the folds of the portières parted and Elsa entered. Her whole manner seemed changed, her radiant brown eyes and her rosy cheeks. Her " Good morning " sounded so fresh and gay, it seemed as if a happy sunbeam entered the room.

" Your father is not well ? " asked Aunt Ratenow pleasantly.

" Unfortunately no, dear aunt. I am going there immediately after breakfast."

" It is thawing," said Moritz ; " put on thick boots."

" And when you return, Elsa, come to my room," added Mrs. von Ratenow.

" A note from Lieutenant Bernardi." The servant came up to Moritz and handed him a note.

Aunt Lott suddenly felt her hand seized by a trembling little hand. Moritz read the note, his face wore a strange expression ; he read it through once, then said, without looking up, " Lieutenant Bernardi presents his best compliments and regrets that he cannot come personally to say farewell, but unfortunately his time is

limited. This evening he leaves at six o'clock for
H—— where he has received the post of command of a
comrade who has been taken ill. He begs that his violin
and music may be given to the messenger, and hopes that
the ladies are well after yesterday's dissipation, and
that they will keep him in friendly remembrance."

" Get the violin from the drawing-room," commanded
Moritz. Then he took a visiting-card from his note-
book, wrote a few words in pencil, put it in an envelope
and handed it to the servant. "Our best regards to
Lieutenant Bernardi."

The two brown eyes gazed at the little violin-case as
if bewitched, as it vanished behind the portières. All was
so still in the room that one could hear only the rattling
of the knife and fork which Mrs. von Ratenow laid on
her plate and picked up again. There is an old saying
that at such times an angel flies through the room, but
this time it was an angel of death who blighted a beautiful flower as yet scarcely opened, which had just
begun to bloom so happily in a young human heart.

At last Moritz resolved to speak. He compelled himself to look at the young, deathly-pale face.

" Well, Elsa, shall we go to the city ? Shall we pur-
chase the children's school-books ? " Involuntarily he
pushed his hand across the table.

" Well, we have sat long enough, children." Mrs.
von Ratenow rose and Elsa left the room ; she wished
to get her things, she said dully.

" For Heaven's sake, the poor child !" said Aunt Lott,

bursting into tears. "She loves him, they love each other."

"Bernardi is a sensible man," declared Mrs. von Ratenow. " Do not cry, Lott," she continued ; " I have long known that it must come so, but an old woman like me has learned by experience that such things can be survived—now it is over."

" Good morning," cried Frieda. "I will go and dress. What a pity that Bernardi is going away ! What will become of our lovely musical evenings ? " She disappeared into the adjoining room. Moritz heard her singing and talking carelessly to her little son.

" Moritz," said Mrs. von Ratenow, " Thomas, the jeweller, has a little enamel bracelet in his show window. Elsa admired it so greatly a few days ago ; buy it, and I will return you the money a few days later. Well, good morning."

" Pray go upstairs, Aunt Lott, and look after the girl," Moritz begged, in nervous haste.

" Is all over, then ? " asked the weeping little lady— " all ? "

" But, dear little auntie, it could not be otherwise."

She turned away and dried her eyes, then she slowly ascended the stairs.

Elsa sat at the window and looked out into the garden ; the snow had melted from the trees, and the branches, black and wet, tossed in the wind. The sky was overcast, a fine mist was rising and obliterating the landscape. Aunt Lott busied herself with the stove ;

the child must not see that she wept, and she picked up the dusting-cloth and wiped the dazzlingly polished furniture on which not a speck of dust lay ; she wished to say something but she did not know what.

The door of the young girl's bedroom stood ajar ; in her embarrassment, the old lady went in there. There stood the bed with its dainty white hangings, the little crucifix of mother-of-pearl which she had brought with her from school hung at the head ; in the corner of the room, near the stove, was the doll-house with all the pretty trifles of her childhood, and on the table, under the mirror, carefully preserved in fresh water, the half-withered bouquet of violets. The clock ticked in the adjoining room, except for that there was utter silence.

Then a door opened and Moritz's voice was heard in the next room, as softly as though he were speaking to a child, " Elsa ! Elsa ! How you look ! What is the matter ? "

" With me ? Nothing at all, Moritz."

" You are our good sensible girl, Elsa."

She started up from her chair. " Say nothing ! Do not speak to me, Uncle Moritz," she cried, and walked past Aunt Lott, who had returned to the sitting-room, and stretched out both hands to her, but she entered her room and closed the door behind her.

He turned to the window. " How sorry I am, Aunt Lott !—There she goes," he remarked after a while; " she has on her coat and hat. I should not have let her go alone. Where can she be going, Aunt Lott ?

She has turned off towards the left, through the garden."

"That is the path she always takes to the churchyard, Moritz; it is nearer, you know; she passes the little chapel."

In fact she was going there. At the moment she had no will of her own. The snow was very soft and walking difficult. All at once she was so tired, so fearfully tired. Not far from the entrance of the churchyard she saw Annie Cramm coming towards her. The young lady had her skates over her arm, and seemed in great haste as she came along the path in her elegant brown skating costume.

" Good morning, Elsa ; how are you ? " She gazed keenly from beneath her veil at the girl's pale face.

" Thank you, Annie ; very well," was the reply.

" Are you going to the churchyard ? Good gracious, what elegiac thoughts so early in the morning, after such a gay evening ! "

Elsa merely nodded.

" I will come with you to the gate, Elsa, if you will permit. You surely know that you have become quite famous over night," said she as they walked on. " Papa came home from the club, and only think, he told it as the greatest news—I laughed myself almost sick over it—that Bernardi has exchanged with Lieutenant P—— because he received the mitten from your aunt or you. I do not know which. I said at once that it was nonsense—Bernardi ! Well, you know, Elsa, and do not be vexed with me, he cannot possibly marry a poor girl."

At this moment the two brown eyes looked at the speaker with such an expression of hopeless misery that the girl paused in alarm and changed her skates from her left to her right hand.

"Well, good-by, Elsa," said she finally. "Perhaps I will come to see you this afternoon. Give my love to Mrs. von Ratenow."

Now Elsa stood at the grave and stared at it, all was so cold and silent ; it was only a grave—dead—like that which lay beneath it ; not a soul was in the church-yard, only a pert little robin redbreast sat there and stared at her with round curious eyes. She had never felt the signification of this grave so fearfully and bitterly as at this hour ; the religious mood, which usually was hers when she came here, would not come to-day. "Why am I alive, why was I not buried with her?" she thought.

"You will take cold here, Miss," said the old sexton, who, his hands in his pockets, came slowly along in his heavy boots. "There is nothing to see now, Miss; but in the spring it will be pretty here; then the blue crocuses which you planted will come up."

She turned away and walked to the city. Her old father was there and he was sick; she had wholly forgotten it in the last few hours, these dreadful hours. On the street she met Lieutenant Rost; he started when he saw her, she was so pale and bowed in such an absent-minded way. For a moment he stood and looked after the slender, girlish form, then, whistling softly, he walked on. He always whistled when anything affected him painfully.

"I am glad you have come, dear Elsa! Oh, your papa, your papa!" Susan whispered to the young girl down in the hall. "There has been no living in the house with him since yesterday when the messenger brought the great letter, and a short time ago the Bennewitzer announced himself, and now he is perfectly furious."

Elsa entered the old man's room. He sat in his arm-chair by the window, his pipe lay on the table, and his hands held a crumpled letter.

"You came at last, Elsa. I might be sick and die here; and yet it was on your account that I had the vexation of this accursed affair."

8

She had no word of reply to his unjust reproof. " I will stay with you, papa, if you wish," said she after a pause.

" No; I do not wish it at all, you know that that cannot be. But I must speak with you ; you must know that there is no longer any justice ; that yesterday I learned that the suit had been decided against me, because— just because it was mine. If the Bennewitzer were I and I he, the bread would, of course, not fall down on the buttered side."

Elsa was silent ; her head ached, and she was so in- different as to what life now had before her.

" But may the devil take me if I will let matters go thus. I shall proceed if I must carry the suit to the highest court of the empire and starve to do it. And what do you think," he continued, striking the table with his clenched fist, "here this man who has not an iota more than I, once more offers me alms and tells me that he will come here to-day to see me ! Would you have considered that possible ? He shall come. Susan shall let him in, I am just in the right mood."

Ah, how terribly hopeless and desolate this life was, this world, where everything depends upon wealth, where even the noblest and purest feeling of the human heart must yield to contemptible interests. The girl felt a loathing of wealth, of the power of money ; her faith, her love, her ideals were trodden in the dust, and she must live. She clasped her forehead with both hands when the old man began to scold again.

"Papa, pray stop!" she begged. "It is all of no matter—I need nothing."

They both were silent. Elsa stood by the stove and gazed about the dingy, smoky room; outside, the melting snow dripped monotonously from the eaves, and occasionally some noise in the street was heard. Now steps, the house door was opened, and the steps came up the stairs. She left the room.

"Stay down-stairs, Mr. von Hegebach," she asked softly, leaning over the banisters.

"Why? I must speak with my cousin."

"Papa is so excited," was the reply.

"You look pale, Miss von Hegebach; will it disturb you if I——"

"Papa is ill, I think," Elsa interposed.

"May I speak with you then, Mademoiselle?'

"With me? Oh, yes; but——"

"Where?"

"Indeed—I do not know——"

Susan came and opened the door. "It is in good order, and not too cold, Elsa."

It was a small room in which they now stood; in the back part stood the old woman's store of apples, a chest gayly painted with flowers, a wardrobe, two spinning-wheels and a reel, while the whole room was fragrant with the fruit. The last rays of the setting sun shone through the little window and fell upon the aristocratic face of the Bennewitzer Hegebach.

"I come to speak once more with your papa; he is

only putting himself to useless exertion and expense, my dear young lady ; be assured that he will obtain nothing by a new suit, and that I deeply pity him——"

" I have not the slightest influence over papa, Mr. von Hegebach," answered Elsa.

" I am sorry for that. But perhaps you can tell him that I am still ready to fulfil my former proposition."

" Papa will accept no money," was the cold reply.

" But why do you take that view of the matter ? " he asked, also becoming cooler. " I merely offer him the interest of a capital which I cannot take out of the estate."

" I know nothing about it, sir," was the answer.

" But you should represent my intentions to your father in his and in your interests, my dear cousin."

" In papa's interests ? He wishes nothing for himself. And I—I thank you very much."

" So speak only girls of your age, who do not yet know what it is to——"

" To have no money, to be poor ? " the young girl interrupted him, and all the bitterness of her heart came from the quivering lips. " I know, Mr. von Hegebach, one learns very soon. If God were just, he would create no poor girls, or he would at least let them come into the world heartless and unfeeling."

Involuntarily he drew back and stared at the little mouth drawn with pain which had· spoken these words.

" Whence comes this bitterness ? " he asked, at length.

"Other girls of your age, at worst, weep when a disappointment befalls them."

"I have no reason to weep," she replied shortly.

"I do not like to go thus, Elsa von Hegebach," he began after a pause; "it seems to me that I do wrong to leave you in this bitter frame of mind. At least promise me that you will consider what I said before; it is no alms, it is your right that is offered to you."

"I do not believe that papa——"

"But you yourself!"

"I? Oh, I have passed my governess's examinations." It was the old tune again. It sounded almost scornful.

"You have your father's obstinacy," he said, taking his hat. "Where must I turn to find some one with some influence over you?"

"I fear you would seek in vain for such a person, Mr. von Hegebach."

"Good-by, Miss von Hegebach." She inclined her head slightly, and he left the house.

When the girl was alone, she leaned her head against the white-washed wall; something like a groan was heard in the little room, and the slender form trembled violently.

"Who was that?" asked the old man irritably, when she returned to him.

"The Bennewitzer, papa."

"And you would not allow him to see me?"

"I told him that you were not well; he wished to offer you the income again."

"Let him go to the—" burst out the old man; "it is the surest proof that he is on an insecure footing."

"Shall I stay with you, papa? Will you have some tea?" she asked.

"No! I am going to bed. I do not feel quite well."

"Let me stay here!" She had come quite near him in the darkness; now her hands rested upon his shoulders.

"What are you thinking of, Elsa? Why do you wish to stay here?" It sounded almost gentle.

"Sometimes I feel that I belong with you, papa."

"Yes, yes! But then I should not be a beggar, child."

"Do I not even then, papa?"

She received no answer. "Listen, Elsa," he said at length, "the Bennewitzer has neither chick nor child, and if there were any justice you should inherit all that fortune some day. But just because you are a girl— the contemptible will expressly states that girls are positively excluded from inheriting."

Suddenly she knelt beside him and laid her head on his hand.

"And," he continued, "it torments me every day that you were not a boy; not for my sake, no, for yours. Your mother cried out in alarm when they told her that you were a girl; we had thought you must positively be a boy. Her last words were, 'Oh, a girl! A poor little girl!' Ah, well, so it is; you must get along as best you can, child. But promise me one thing—when I am dead—I have indeed done nothing to make you love me much, every one else has done more for you, the Rate-now and Moritz; but one cannot choose one's father in this world, Elsa."

"No, papa, and I cannot help it that I am a poor girl," said she, childishly. And two large tears rolled down on to the old man's hand.

"Do not cry, child, pray do not cry!" He was nervous again. "And you must go, Elsa; it is dark already."

She rose and looked for hat and cloak. "Sleep well, papa. I will come again when I have time. I begin my lessons to-morrow."

She walked down the dark dirty street; usually she had always been afraid at this time of the evening, to-day she did not think of it. The wind had risen and howled through the long alley, and the fine rain cooled her cheeks and eyes.

She walked as slowly as though it were a May evening. A carriage suddenly turned through the castle gate and drove past her at a rapid pace ; it was the Bennewitzer's carriage. He must have paid Aunt Ratenow a visit, perhaps to find in her an ally.

"I wish that I could die," she thought. She must return to the house, and yet she would prefer to run away as far as her feet could carry her.

"Miss von Hegebach, you are to go at once to the mistress," said the servant in the vestibule. She gave him her hat and cloak, and went directly.

Mrs. von Ratenow sat on the sofa ; a decanter and two glasses stood on the table, and the fragrance of a fine cigar still scented the air. "How is your father?" she asked, and motioned to the girl to be seated.

"I thank you, he is not well, aunt."

"You look pale, that is from dancing, Elsa."

"Yes, aunt."

"Listen, there comes the little mouse," said the old lady, smiling at the pretty child who crossed the room with an expression of solemn importance and went up to Elsa. "From grandmama, auntie," she whispered, and laid something heavy in the young girl's lap, then quickly ran back to her hiding-place. It was a pretty enamel bracelet which Elsa held in her hand.

"You are so good, dear aunt," said she, gazing at her with her beautiful brown eyes. They were no longer child's eyes since this morning, and she kissed the offered hand. " I will wear it in remembrance of you."

" I was about to ask you to do so, Elsa. And now go—the Bennewitzer left his regards for you."

Having reached her room, she hastily put away the bracelet. She wished no pity, she could not endure it, she thought. As though an ornament could cure her heartache and bitter longing. She would gladly have kept her room, but then they would think she was weeping for him, and she would not shed a tear, not one.

But it could not be thus. Suddenly she inhaled a sweet perfume, a perfume which only yesterday had almost intoxicated her. There stood the violets, *his* violets, and it seemed as though they spoke with his voice, " Happiness ! What is happiness if not this moment ?" Suddenly she sobbed loudly ; it sounded like a cry of pain, and the next moment the room door opened and Aunt Lott held the quivering girl in her arms.

Aunt Lott knew all ; she might also see that her heart was broken, quite broken.

IX.

ABOUT two weeks had passed, when one morning Aunt Lott went down-stairs and asked for Moritz. The servant told her that he was with his wife, so the old lady crossed Frieda's blue drawing-room and asked, pausing behind the portières, "Do I disturb you, children?"

"Come in, Aunt Lott!" cried Moritz.

Frieda sat at the writing-desk. "One moment, aunt," said she, and once more glanced over the sheet of note paper adorned with her crest.

"MY DEAREST LILI:

"Only a few words in the greatest haste so that you may be *au fait* as regards my ball costume for Berlin, as we will soon be together. I have ordered of Gerson a white satin gown embroidered in silver, the corsage of *drap d'argent*, and shall wear my diamonds with it instead of flowers. I think it will have quite a distinguished look. Mamma and Moritz insist upon taking with them Elsa, who, of late, has been more than tiresome, *à cause de Monsieur Bernardi*. Mamma has ordered a pink silk gown for her. I have had more than enough of this Elizabeth worship, and mean to express my opinion to Moritz thoroughly. I earnestly beg you, Lili, never to take into your house a young girl who has certain family rights, it is more than annoying ; especially when the master of the house feels under as great obligations to play the fatherly protector and knight as Moritz. My patience will not last much longer. Give my love to father and mother. *Auf Wiedersehen.*

" Your Sister,   FRIEDA.

" P. S.—The Bennewitzer comes remarkably often now. I do not trust my mother-in-law on this subject ; she says on Elsa's father's account. There is an old proverb—but I will not write it down here.

" F."

" Now, auntie, what is it ? " she asked, after sealing and addressing the letter. And she went to a charming little cabinet, drew out different drawers, and prepared to inspect her jewels. She wore a pale-blue *négligé*, and upon her luxuriant black hair rested a lace rosette with blue ribbons.

" Oh, dear," began Aunt Lott, turning to Moritz, who sat motionless beside the fire, in his rough suit and heavy boots, just as he had come from the fields. " Oh, dear, Moritz, I am so worried about Elsa—she does not complain, she says nothing, but she does not sleep at all, she eats nothing, and grows so thin. Will you not send the doctor upstairs when he comes ? I am afraid she will torment herself sick about this Bernardi."

" Is the comedy not at an end yet ? " asked the young wife. What will you have ? Elsa seems highly satisfied. That she is a little bit shy about going out is natural ; she was the talk of the town for a week."

" Yes, she is very reserved, Frieda," said the old lady, nodding gravely, " but——"

" Well, you do all you can to console her," continued
Frieda irritably, and replaced a costly gem in its box
somewhat roughly. " No one asks whether I am suited
now, everything is Elsa. Mamma does so, and the children and Moritz. I may not even express a wish, and
after this I shall not say another word at the table."

Aunt Lott looked fairly in alarm at Moritz, who
leaned back in his chair so indifferently.

" Auntie, Frieda knows that it is very becoming to
her to pout a little. But you must not take this bad
temper with us to Berlin, child, or else——"

" If you insist upon taking Elsa with you, I shall stay
here with my bad temper," she interrupted.

" You must arrange that with mother," said he calmly ;
"she wishes that Elsa should accompany us."

" I cannot take her on account of the children," per-
sisted his wife. " I really do not see why I should have
a governess if I cannot once leave home in peace."

" Up to this time, the old nurse has always been sufficient to take charge of them. But as you will, Frieda.
I have never quarrelled with you when it pleased you
to put on your defiant little mood, you know it. To-day
is the last day in which Elsa shall act as governess. I
will take steps this very hour to engage another lady."

Frieda was silent, and closed one drawer after another
very slowly.

" I only beg you to be considerate, Frieda," he began
again, " do not let the girl suspect the cause of this arrangement. The rest will take care of itself."

He had risen, took cap and riding whip from the nearest chair, and left the room. In the same moment the young wife buried her face in her hands and burst into tears.

"Oh, Aunt Lott, I am so very unhappy!"

The good old lady did not know what to make of this scene. "For Heaven's sake, Frieda, what is the matter with you?"

"He no longer loves me!" sobbed the beautiful woman, and threw herself into an arm-chair. "I know it too well, he loves me no longer!"

" Good heavens, you surely are not jeal—— ? " The frightened spinster could not utter the whole word.

" And now he will go to mamma—to mamma, who always treats me like a silly child ! "

Suddenly she started up ; the blue curtains were parted, and Mrs. von Ratenow, in all her stateliness, entered the room.

" Well, Frieda, I just heard from Moritz that you are not feeling quite well," she began, seating herself beside the weeping young woman.

Frieda stammered something about a headache.

" Of course ! " The old lady took her hand. " The noise of the children all day long is too much for you. I know that nerves are the fashion nowadays. But I will make you a proposition : Send the little girls to school ; the house will be delightfully quiet then, my little daughter, and you need no longer worry yourself with a governess, eh ? "

The young wife started up from her reclining position, but could not answer.

" Elsa Hegebach shall remain here as my companion, dear child," continued the old lady, raising her voice ; " and as such I will know how to protect her from all insult, Frieda ! "

Frieda had paled slightly. " I did not mean it so," said she, beginning to cry again.

" Where is Elsa ? " asked her mother-in-law.

" In the nursery ; she is giving the children an arithmetic lesson," was the reply in a low tone.

"I hope to see you at tea this evening," continued Mrs. von Ratenow. "Pray be punctual, Aunt Lott. The Bennewitzer is coming."

"The third time in two weeks," remarked Frieda, rising. "He never used to come, or at least very seldom."

"Certainly. For years he had an invalid wife, and until recently he has been in deep mourning. Shall I have the pleasure of seeing you at tea this evening?" she asked once more.

"I am very sorry, dear mamma, we are invited to tea at Mrs. von Z——'s."

"Elsa too?"

"Elsa was invited, but declined."

"Then I trust she will accept my invitation." And the old lady nodded to her daughter-in-law most pleasantly. "Good morning, my dear child; send the children to me for a little while, if you like."

"Do you see, auntie, mamma is always like that," complained Frieda. "Any one will admit that I am right. If Elsa undertakes to educate the children she should do it entirely. I am the last person to demand anything exorbitant of her. If I lose my patience it is no wonder. I fancy the children will at last learn something; and Moritz comes and says: 'Elsa, we are going to the subscription ball in Berlin; mother will give you a dress.' How are the lessons to continue in earnest?"

"I think Elsa did not wish to accept your offer, Frieda." The anxious old lady defended her *protégé.*

But she was forced to listen to a long lament. Frieda considered her rights so deeply infringed upon she even fulfilled her threat, and did not utter a syllable at dinner.

Thus a storm which had long threatened Moritz's domestic happiness burst ; the atmosphere of the house was oppressive despite the clear, frosty weather outside. Elsa did not notice it ; she had a little girl on either side, and was sufficiently occupied in answering the children's questions. At first Moritz had not wished the children to come to the dinner-table, but Elsa had thought it best that they should, so they were permitted to their great delight.

She did, indeed, look miserable, and she was very quiet ; this was the result of her combat with a proud, injured heart, which incessantly asked, " Why ? " This was the result of the sleepless nights and tormenting longing for the lost golden days. She seemed to herself a pariah among the others, hopeless and repulsive, and only because—she was poor ! Her brown eyes might not even weep, like those of the poor girl in the song. But still there was much in the world that made life desirable ; hundreds and hundreds had shared her fate, and had yet become calm and content through hard work—without happiness. But the path of all these had gone through thorns and thistles ; a young, wounded heart, thirsting for happiness, could not find forgetfulness in a few days ; years, long years, were required for that.

In the evening old Mrs. von Ratenow's room was the coseyest in the whole house ; the tea-kettle sang and hummed in every key ; the heavy curtains were drawn before the windows, keeping out every draught ; the lamp-light was reflected in the shining silver and glass on the snow-white damask table-cloth ; and Aunt Lott and the owner sat on the sofa, the latter her white knitting in her hand. Elsa, busy with some dainty work, sat near the alcohol lamp, above which hung the kettle ; she wore a dark house-gown and a delicately embroidered apron. The Bennewitzer was expected.

These hours with the old gentleman were fairly horrible to Elsa ; her feelings were too varied. Since her father had recently spoken his first pleasant words to her, her childish heart had gone out in passionate love to the surly man. She knew that he had not treated his cousin well, but he had said that he did it for her sake, and in the eyes of the girl that excused everything, his moods, his obstinacy, the slight interest in herself. He had long since again become unfriendly as ever to her, but she had had one glance into his embittered nature ; now no word was too harsh, no mood too gloomy for her ; the dross of grief and soli- tude merely covered the golden heart of the old man ; he was her father, the only being upon whom she had a claim, a sacred right.

The Bennewitzer's presence therefore was painful to her. Up to this time he had never spoken in the castle of his visit to her father ; but, nevertheless, she knew

9

what he thought of him, and that pained her unspeakably. Besides Aunt Ratenow praised the Bennewitzer so uncommonly. Aunt Ratenow had such pronounced likes and dislikes, and one must oppose nothing to these, for the old lady could then raise her voice so loudly. "Good or bad, there is nothing between," she often remarked. There was no medium for her, it was foreign to her whole character. Bernardi's name never passed her lips; the affair was ended once for all, the less it was discussed the better. A wound must bleed, she thought, but that could happen secretly without attracting notice.

"Elsa," she began in her deep voice—she pushed back her spectacles and let the paper fall—"you may read aloud to me, my eyes grow daily worse. I do not know, Lottie, how you have preserved yours with your eternal reading. It is a true comfort to me that Moritz has yielded to my request, and taken the instruction of the children from you, Elsa. I am really able neither to read the paper in the morning nor to write a letter except in a wretched scrawl."

Elsa took the paper. "If I were only sure, dear aunt, that Moritz and Frieda were not dissatisfied with me as a teacher."

"Oh, that is what people always say when they wish to be complimented," replied the old lady. "No, no, it is not that; I begged Moritz to do it. How do you think a person fares when she cannot see well? But there comes the Bennewitzer!" she interrupted herself.

A carriage rolled across the yard and stopped before the door. Steps were heard in the hall, and Mrs. von Ratenow rose with a certain solemnity.

"Good evening, my dear Hegebach!" cried she, shaking his hand vigorously. "I am glad that you come to enliven three lonely women."

He kissed the offered hand politely, and bowed to Aunt Lott and Elsa. To the latter he gave a white paper parcel.

"The only one in the conservatory," he said courteously. It was a magnificent Marshal Niel; the beautiful yellow flower nodded heavily on its graceful stem.

"Thank you very much, Mr. von Hegebach."

She placed the rose in a little vase, and busied herself about the tea-table.

"Is there any news, dear Mr. Hegebach?" asked Mrs. von Ratenow; and with that conversation was started. Both knew all the countryside, and from that they came to old times.

"Pardon, dear Hegebach, I am ten years older than you; just as old as your cousin, I know very well."

"No, you are mistaken, my dear madam," he declared, very calmly. "At most you are but eight years older. I was thirty-six when I married, and that was eighteen years ago. Remember that my poor eldest boy was in the third class at school."

"True; how time passes, Hegebach!"

"To be sure, to be sure. Elsa will be nineteen this spring," said Aunt Lott.

"Well, there are older people than we, Hegebach ; you are really still a young man," said Mrs. von Ratenow.

Aunt Lott glanced at him ; he was aristocratic, stately, still handsome, but young? She had long ceased to consider herself young, yet she was not many years his senior. "Men always have the advantage of us," thought she.

Elsa sat there quietly, her thoughts were quite different. What did she care about old, long-forgotten stories? All those lay so far behind her. A nervous uneasiness took possession of her as was so often the case. She would gladly have gone up to her little room, seated herself at the window, and thought and dreamed ; it was so very hard not to give way to her sad, longing thoughts, but be forced to answer and listen.

"How is your father?" asked the Bennewitzer, and leaned toward Elsa.

"Thank you, not very well I think," she replied.

"And not yet in a milder frame of mind?" He spoke softly and his dark eyes gazed into hers pleadingly.

She suddenly blushed. "Papa does not change his views over night," said she roughly and loudly.

Mrs. von Ratenow's face darkened. "Elsa, please pour tea."

The young girl rose, crossed the soft carpet noiselessly, and disappeared into the next room. Baron von

Hegebach's eyes followed her, he stroked his dark beard slowly with his white, well-cared-for hand. Mrs. von Ratenow spoke of something else, she apparently wished to make him forget the rough answer. When the young girl returned, they were chatting animatedly.

Baron von Hegebach was an excellent companion ; he had travelled extensively, he knew a number of distinguished, famous people. He spoke of Lapland and Lebanon, and he talked well. He had everywhere seen the best ; he had raved over the Nile and sketched it ; he had stood by the falls of Niagara. He was a man who knew the pleasantest side of life. And there, in the gloomy house, sat a solitary old man who did not even have the money necessary for travelling expenses, that he might visit a cure for the relief of his sufferings. What his cousin had paid in Cairo for a single dagger would have been sufficient for several weeks' stay in Teplitz.

Hateful, angry thoughts were hidden behind Elsa's white forehead. All in which she had formerly believed, love, fidelity, nobility, were absurdities, long since out of date. To-day but one thing conferred happiness, power—money, wealth.

" To our good friendship, dear little cousin ! " The Bennewitzer raised his glass. She touched hers to it.

" Will you not look at me ? " said he gravely.

Again her face flushed crimson, she was vexed with herself, but those eyes wore such a strange expression.

" Stay here, Elsa ! " cried Mrs. von Ratenow, as the

Bennewitzer drove away about eleven o'clock, not without having received a promise that the ladies would soon visit him at Bennewitz

Elsa returned and seated herself again. Aunt Lott had already taken leave at the stroke of ten.

Mrs. von Ratenow looked vexed, but did not know how to begin. "You have a strange way of treating the Bennewitzer, dear child," said she, at length. "It is absurd to lay up against him a suit which your father was foolish enough to enter into ; you should at least be neutral."

"I know that Baron von Hegebach is entirely in the right, aunt," said Elsa, gazing directly at the old lady. "I do not lay up anything against him, that would be foolish."

"Very well! But why are you so—so repellent to him ? "

"I beg pardon, aunt—" she stammered.

Mrs. von Ratenow rose and gave her her hand. " I do not know whether you are different from others— you are not usually one of those whom it is hard to make understand. Good-night, Elsa ! "

The girl rushed upstairs to her room as if chased. No, it was not possible, her aunt could not possibly have meant what flashed through her mind at that moment. But what else ? She laughed aloud, but it was a scornful laugh, it sounded strangely even to her. Then she stood before the mirror and gazed at her pale face. Certainly it was absurd, only her excitement

could make her imagine such foolishness. No, aunt
had meant nothing ; it had been merely a common form
of speech, naturally.

" Aunt Lott," she then called softly. It seemed as
though she were afraid of her own thoughts, and she
went into the old lady's painfully neat bedroom.

"What is it, my darling ?" was the sleepy query.

" I feel so timid, aunt."

And Aunt Lott sat up in bed good-naturedly.

" This evening I was so reminded of your mother,
child," she began. " We always sat in cousin Ratenow's
room when your father came a-courting her. You resemble her so greatly, Elsa, and yet have a likeness to
the Bennewitzer and your father—the voice and gesture
—but the beard, you know, and then he always looked
at her in silence."

The girl stood motionless ; an inexplicable anxiety
contracted her throat.

"It is almost twenty years since then, and yet it
seems like to-day to me, Elsa," the old lady continued,
in her complaining tearful manner; " only that Aunt
Ratenow has grown much stouter and that my hair has
turned white. How vivid the past sometimes becomes!
Lieschen, your mother, always came to my bedside
then, and once, I remember very well, she said, " Lottie,
Lottie, I feel so timid."

"Aunt, pray stop—I am frightened." The slender
girlish figure, which stood close beside the bed, shook
as with a nervous chill.

" You are not well, Elsa."

" No, I believe I am going to be ill, aunt."

" Poor child—that is from your grieving."

" I do not grieve, aunt."

" I know very well, child, but one does it without wishing. When the doctor comes to-morrow he shall give you something to make you sleep; I have spoken to Moritz already. Or do you think I do not notice how late into the night you read? I hear every page turned. Good-night, my darling child, go to sleep. Formerly, I could always sit up late, but now——"

X.

WEEKS had passed; it was spring. For a long time a hateful east wind had blown, chilling to the bones those whom the clear blue sky and golden sunlight enticed out of doors, so that they shut themselves up in their houses in disgust, and the flowers regretted that they had ventured out so prematurely. But now a warm, fragrant spring breeze blew, gray clouds chased each other across the sky, and sunshine and rain came by turns. The buds were bursting on all the bushes, in the castle garden the lawn was blue with violets, and in the church-yard blue crocuses bloomed on Elsa's · mother's grave.

She had just hung a wreath upon the cross which bore the name of the dead ; to-day was the anniversary of her mother's death, and was also her birthday, a thorn in the girl's wreath of life, a dark spot which so closely allied her existence to the dead. For a long time she sat on the stone coping which surrounded the grave, and her hands mechanically arranged the leaves of the wreath, while her eyes gazed over all the crosses and stones into space.

Her life had now become an eternal wordless conflict with herself, with every one else; she no longer possessed any one in whom she could confide. All had taken part against her, even Moritz. She felt it; Moritz had something against her, he avoided her, and Frieda was so terribly heartless.

"She has never had a trouble in her life," said Aunt Ratenow; "she is a spoiled child, and one should not pay much attention to them, as children can never really insult grown people."

But Aunt Lott had suddenly gone to Z——. One day she had come out of Aunt Ratenow's room with tearful eyes, and had packed her trunk. The stern cousin had said that she thought it more practical this year for Lott to spend the summer at home, so Lott was now passing her prescribed eight weeks in the cloister. For what Aunt Ratenow commanded must be done.

Frieda's sister Lili was visiting her. She was a little brunette, not as pretty as her sister, but with such a merry laugh, and she knew how to turn the whole house topsy-turvy even better than Frieda.

Mrs. von Ratenow declared that she was a new-fashioned feather-head, and it was well that she and Annie Cramm were friends, they were quite suited to each other. But in spite of her many social distractions, Miss Lili always appeared at "dear, charming" Madame von Ratenow's tea-table, she was so fond of old ladies and gentlemen, and she should never fall in love with a young man. She preferred men in the fifties, and how interesting for a young woman to have an old husband! It was very droll to hear her talk thus; and against her will Mrs. von Ratenow must smile.

"But he must have a great deal of money, eh, Lili?"

"Of course, dearest, best of aunts, either a great deal of money, or he must at least be an Excellency, general, or something similar."

And the Bennewitzer came so very often now, and Aunt Ratenow was more charming than ever to him. "Elsa, his is a fine character." And Frieda always had a sweet smile for him, and Lili raised her long lashes so slowly as she talked to him. There was a perfect race when his elegant carriage rolled into the yard. Aunt Ratenow met him with great dignity in the hall. Frieda and Lili stood on the stairs, and poor Mr. von Hegebach was seriously embarrassed because he did not know whether to enter Frieda's cosey boudoir or Aunt Ratenow's sober room; but in any case, let him turn where he would, he drew the whole company after him.

And Elsa apparently stood without this circle, and yet knew unmistakably that she became more and more the central point. Again and again she tried to win back every inch of ground forced from her, unconsciously her eyes rested piteously upon her aunt's stern face; her heart started back in affright at the gaze of a man's two dark eyes, as day by day she lost more and more of her firm footing.

This morning, her birthday, a beautiful bouquet had stood on the table for her in Aunt Ratenow's room, and the card attached bore the giver's name. A letter from Aunt Lott, dear old Aunt Lott, was also there. Moritz had pressed her hand and brought her a pretty portfolio of Russia leather, and then the children had clung to her joyously. Lili and Frieda also had appeared, the latter with all sorts of ribbons, scarfs, and "such non-

sense," as Aunt Ratenow called it; and one pale-blue sash the old lady had returned to her, with the remark that that had probably only been given with the other things by accident, and belonged to Frieda's toilet-table, as the pins still sticking in it proved.

But Elsa was so weary, it was quite indifferent to her
if Frieda wished to pass off old things upon her; she
was only a poor girl, why should she not wear cast-off
sashes ? She had no money for these " sweet trifles of
life," as Moritz loved to call his beautiful wife's costly
frippery ; it was only natural in Frieda, she did not
mean unkindly. Ah, if they had demanded nothing
more of her !

Aunt Ratenow had told her this morning of the day
of her birth, and how sad it had been, how since that
time her father had become a gloomy, lonely man; and
she had told him that the child would yet be a blessing
to him, a great blessing.

" And that is in your power, Elsa," she had added.

The young girl rose from her seat in the quiet ceme-
tery, the icy, horrible feeling had again come over her.
Hastily she walked along the path ; she did not see how
brightly the sun shone, how its rays sparkled in the dew-
drops which clung to the tender young leaves ; everywhere was spring—young, green, and the gay twitter
of birds ; a slender pale-green branch even rested over
the venerable top of the gateway tower.

Her cheeks were flushed feverishly when she entered
her father's room. She would turn to him ; he hated
the Bennewitzer ; he would permit her to seek refuge
with him, if— The old man had both windows
opened wide, the newspapers lay on the table before
him, and near the cold pipe stood a half-emptied wine-
glass.

" Papa, are you not well ? " asked Elsa.

"Oh, yes, child ! Only my cough and lack of breath—now it is much better, you can shut the window again. I can no longer bear excitement, and to-day—" He held out his hand, and for a moment clasped the slender hand firmly in his.

" Draw the curtains together, the sun shines in here so glaringly, Elsa ; and then—perhaps it will please you —that little chest yonder your mother always had on her sewing-table, and she kept all the little sacques and caps which she made for you in it. I hunted it up, Elsa ; take it with you. It was so pleasant when she sat before it, it was like a bright spot in my life, it all comes back to me on such days. One day she went out, it was Christmas time, and then afterward, when she sat at her sewing-table again, her brown eyes looked at me so happily. ' Hegebach, I saw such a lovely rock-ing-horse at Lehmann, the saddler's ! ' Yes, Elsa, if I could have bought you a rocking-horse all would have been different ! "

The girl lowered her eyes. Still the same refrain !

" And then, child—" he pushed the little mahogany chest with the simple silver plate on the top and the dead mother's name upon it—" then, I have withdrawn the suit against the Bennewitzer."

" Papa ! " It sounded like a cry of alarm.

" Yes, child. Should I not ? You have often told me that I had no right to bring it."

" Yes, papa ; forgive me." She spoke hopelessly.

"And now he wishes to be reconciled to me, Elsa; it was to be a surprise for you, child; they are coming for me to-day with the carriage, we are to drive there together—to Madame Ratenow's, I mean; but I do not know, Elsa, whether it can be. I can bear no excitement, and then it is such an old antipathy, it is not too easy. I know very well that I must do it for your sake, but——"

"Papa! In Heaven's name not for my sake!" begged the girl, white to her very lips. "Who told you that?"

"The Ratenow, child; and she is right, yes, she is right!"

Elsa sprang up from her chair; she tried to speak.

"Do not be vexed, Elsa, that I have betrayed it, for I am so glad. Child, it is a dreadful feeling for a father to be forced to leave his child utterly alone in the world."

"Dear, dear papa!" Her pale face bent down to him. "I am not afraid, certainly not; and you are alive and will live a long time yet, and I may stay with you, papa. I came here to make this request, papa."

"Do not make me weak, Elsa! This has all had such an effect upon me, and Susan is disagreeable and noisy, I—" He suddenly groaned and clutched at his breast. "This stupid oppression—it is well that it has all come about so for you, Elsa! You have no idea of how solitary, cold and dreadful life can be, or else you

would not be so courageous. Life as yet is all roses for
you."

She was silent as if petrified ; she knew now that she
had no one who understood her. At this moment
Susan rushed in in the greatest excitement. The lady
from the castle and the Bennewitzer gentleman were
coming upstairs.

So they had come. The old man in the arm-chair
changed color. "Go into the next room, Elsa, you
need not see how——"

She went into the room which had once been her
mother's, and stood before Mrs. von Ratenow.

"We have come here, Elsa ; at home the very walls
have ears now ; Lili is everywhere, and she need not hear
everything. I do not know how that witch can pursue
Hegebach as she does ; it is probably the fashion now
to pay court to men." And she seated herself in her
heavy silk mantle in the chair by the window, and un-
tied her bonnet-strings.

"Good mercy, how hot old Susan keeps this house ! "
she then added.

Yes, it was suffocating here, so thought the pale girl
yonder, panting for breath. In the other room was
heard the Bennewitzer's sonorous voice, so mild, so
conciliating ; and the old lady by the window played
calmly with her large, well-kept hands. Her face wore
an expression of the utmost satisfaction.

"Listen, Elsa," said she : "nineteen years ago you
lay in this sofa corner and cried piteously. Yes, if one

could know everything beforehand I should not have taken you in my arms with such a heavy heart."

"What do you mean, aunt?"

"Yes, my girl, this is a strange world; the dear God has his own ways, but it all comes about. What do I mean? Oh, nonsense, Elsa; you are no ordinary girl who simpers up to the very last. I know that that question was unnecessary, because secretly you can answer it very accurately. And when you do so with your clear common-sense you should say, 'Thank God! old Aunt Ratenow was, to be sure, always very good to me, but still I had to suit myself to all kinds of moods, it was merely an assistance in time of need; and my old father can now have a few happy, untroubled days!' Eh, my dear?"

"Aunt, I beg you!" gasped the young girl.

"And then, child, he is so good, so very good; he is really a charming man! I will confess to you, Elsa, when I heard—you were still at school then—that he had lost his sons, I thought at once, he will marry again, and then I thought it would be a guidance of the dear God if you should please him, Elsa. I saw it coming gradually with sincere joy, and—now he is in there, Elsa, and asks your father's consent. Come here, child, close to me. Do you think I did not notice the little affair with your handsome young Lieutenant? Oh, Elsa, I too have been young. Lieutenants, child, are very nice for you girls to dance with, but in marriage more is needed than two bright eyes and

10

shining epaulettes! Elsa, how can any one look so rigid? Why, Elsa!"

The girl had sunk down and raised her clasped hands.

"Aunt, aunt, have pity!" she sobbed with tearless eyes. "I will do everything—I will—I cannot!"

"Merciful heavens!" She seized the girl around the waist and raised her. "Elsa, control yourself! More is

at stake than a girlish fancy. Refrain from that ' I
cannot ! ' my child. Life is earnest, very earnest, one
cannot look at it through colored glasses, the welfare of
a whole life is involved. This is no leap into a bed of
roses, it should be a serious step, taken with honest will
and firm resolve. I should have fared but ill, my child,
had I not had a wise father. Do you think I would
have chosen Frederick Ratenow ? No, Elsa. I was
head over ears in love with a very, very poor wretch of
a candidate who was my brother's tutor. I was a bold
thing, and told my father so when Ratenow asked for
my hand. Gracious, child, you should have seen !
Before I could turn around, the candidate was out of
the house and Ratenow's ring was on my finger. And
what would you have ? It is so with every princess !
No, no, Elsa ; be sensible."

She stroked the blonde head which rested so quietly
on her breast. " You will be sensible, eh ? "

" Not now, aunt ! Give me time, I implore you ! "
begged the trembling girl. " I must first become
calmer—you must grant me this, you must ! "

She spoke the last passionately. The old lady saw
that she could press the excited girl no more.

" Listen, child ; take a walk, there is time before
dinner." She went and fetched the girl's hat and
cloak. " Go, my girl, and may God bless you."

She went, she fairly ran. Outside at least she could
breathe fresh air, and before her lay the broad land.
She yet cherished one hope, she yet felt strong enough

to defend it against the whole world. She thought of the quiet little village in Thuringia, the pretty little church, and the people who lived so peacefully together. She saw Sister Beata's good face under the cap of their order—there was one spot where the storms of life did not reach.

She was at home before she realized it ; she was glad when the servant told her that the ladies were all out. She started upstairs, then suddenly turned.

" Where is the Baron ? "

" In his room, Miss."

She came down-stairs again and knocked at his door.

" Come in."

" Moritz, may I come in ? "

" Why, Elsa, of course ! "

" I wished to ask you something, Moritz."

" Certainly, Elsa. But come, we will go out in the garden."

She looked at him in surprise ; he acted so strangely, as if embarrassed.

" As you will, Moritz."

They went into the garden, and walked up and down the sunny central path. There was a delightful perfume of violets in the air, and above them the birds sang sweetly ; it was a lovely spot, this old castle garden.

Elsa suddenly raised her green fan to her eyes.

" Moritz," she began, " have I offended you in any way ? "

" No, my dear child," he replied gently.

" I thought I must have, you have been so changed
to me for some time."

He watched her as she walked beside him with lowered eyes. What had become of the fresh, blooming
girl ?

" Moritz ! " It was the old, childish tone. " Must
I do what they all wish, must I ? "

" Must ? No, Elsa, but perhaps it would be well for
you to do so."

" I cannot, Moritz."

" Elsa! " He stood still and took her hand. " Think
no more of Bernardi," said he, in his kindly way; " do
not wait for him. Listen, we men forget anything of
that kind. You must not fancy that he torments himself as you do, child, you know nothing of life as yet."

She looked at him again with her mournful eyes, and
a slight flush rose to her pale face.

" I often think of him, Moritz, often, although against
my will, but from the first moment I have hoped no
longer. I know only too well that a chasm, a yawning
chasm, lies between us. I only wonder whether—but
you probably do not understand me, Moritz. I have
not a particle of love for my cousin, not a particle—
such as one should have for—for——"

She stammered, broke off, and stood before him,
blushing deeply, and slowly great tears rolled from
beneath her lowered lashes.

He did understand her, but what should he say ?
What was to become of her ? He could offer her a

home no longer if she refused the Bennewitzer. His
mother would be bitterly angry with her, and Frieda?
His domestic happiness was at stake ; it sounded ridic-

ulous, but the little woman was jealous, really and truly
jealous, and she showed it at every opportunity.   Elsa,
the innocent child, suspected nothing of this, and she
should not learn of it.

He was still silent.

"Elsa," he said at length—and he felt how commonplace his words were—"do not make your life so fearfully hard. Listen—" and he again began to walk up and down, his hands behind his back—"as we grow older and calmer, in later life, we think so differently of love affairs and marriages of affection—what was I going to say?—Elsa, dear, I really would consider the matter."

She did not answer and dried her tears. "Well then, Moritz, I beg you one favor at least, ask Aunt Ratenow not to desire my decision to-day, not to-day. And you, Moritz, forgive me for asking this of you."

She turned and went back to the house. She took the way through the hall; she had heard Frieda's voice in the garden-room and a waltz being played. Lili, as was her wont, played a few bars, only immediately after to begin something else. Elsa reached her little room unobserved, and seated herself by the window. Now she had no friend here, she was alone, they all were angry with her because she scorned an assured future, a comfortable existence, the envied lot of a wealthy young wife, for the one reason which the world thinks so absurd, but which is so sacredly serious for a pure womanly heart. But papa, poor lonely old papa, said an inner voice, the only one which rose in contradiction to her thoughts. "No," said she aloud, "I do not love him, I deceive him and myself." She did not know the outer world with its thorny paths, which a solitary girl must

follow, but it could not be as dreadful as if she—
She sprang up and a nervous shudder overcame her.
Hastily she seized a book and turned over the pages.
Then her eyes rested upon a poem :

> "The mother said, ' My Elsa dear,
>   You must no longer tarry.
>   'Tis possible e'en without love
>   Quite happily to marry.
>   And many a one who marries thus,
>   Merely for home or splendor,
>   Yet thinks herself a happy wife
>   Without this love so tender.' "

She smiled painfully and closed the book; resting her
head on her clasped hands, she wept for the first time
in many a long day like a child—like a poor, deserted
child.   Hours passed, twilight fell, and the moon's
pale light shone into the young girl's room, but still
she sat there in the same position.

Music sounded from the drawing-room ; Miss Lili
was playing the piano to pass the time.   The others
stayed so very long in Aunt Ratenow's room, and the
old lady even requested in the politest manner that
Miss Lili would not come with the others.   It was unbearably tiresome to-day.   Even the dinner with the
Bennewitzer, who had scarcely spoken a word and
merely continually stroked his dark beard, which was
a frequent gesture of his, and before that the family
scene at the Cramms', Annie as a happy *fiancée*, stiff
as a wax-doll, and beside her Lieutenant von Rost,

who looked as utterly indifferent as though the whole affair really did not concern him in the slightest. The only one really affected was Mamma Cramm, for papa's mood seemed rather the result of the silver-necked bottles in the wine-cooler than delight over his son-in-law. As soon as her first astonishment was over, Lili had at once taken leave of the family group, having received permission to tell the happy news everywhere.

Outside, in the hall, she had asked in truly military style : "Annie, when did the bomb burst ? Since when has this been going on ? No one has noticed anything of it until now."

And Annie had blushed. "Oh, we have been fond of each other for a long time, but papa would never hear of it."

"How dreadful !" Lili had suppressed her laughter with difficulty. "But now ?"

"Ah, Lili, I should have died without him."

"Dear me !" cried the rogue in surprise. "Ah, well, I will no longer disturb you. Tell me, Annie, his name is *von* Rost, is it not ?"

"Yes, von Rost." The answer was somewhat short.

"Good-by, Annie !" She had run away, suppressing a giggle with great difficulty, to tell the great news to the household at dinner, and found only displeased faces, and except Frieda no one had taken the slightest interest in the matter.

XI.

AFTER dinner, the Bennewitzer had at once taken leave ; the sisters had gone to the window to look after the handsome carriage, and Lili yawned heartily, then hummed a few bars from *Der Freischutz :*

> "Though he's old, yet he suits me;
> His many wrinkles I'll not see."

And had finished with, "Brr, Frieda! I think I will soon return home."

"Yes. I cannot blame you."

The young wife was cross, and had buried her woes in a novel by Heyse. Moritz had gone to his mother, finally Frieda also.

"Listen, Lili," she had said. "All is not right upstairs. I am going to investigate." The young wife had been gone an eternity already, and Lili was greatly bored; even the pale Elsa did not come to take pity on her.

It was best that she should go home ; there at least she could amuse herself with the master of hounds of the P—— court ; he was far less tiresome than the Ben-

newitzer. Oh, well, what was to be done with such
heroes as the Bennewitzer and Moritz, the great good-
natured bear—and of whom Frieda was so frightfully
jealous—good heavens !

Frieda had first listened at the door, and then gone
in.

Mrs. von Ratenow, calm as ever, sat in her chair
by the window ; the cup, with her coat of arms upon
it, stood beside her as usual, and her hands held her
knitting. Moritz walked up and down the room in
great strides ; he looked excited.

"Ah !" cried the beautiful little woman. "Moritz
is like a wild animal. What has happened ? "

"I am not quite of mamma's opinion, Frieda."

"Indeed," said his wife ironically. "That is certainly unusual."

"And I assert," declared Mrs. von Ratenow, "that
one must be firm ; there are many people who fight
against their happiness as a sick child against medicine."

"And I assert, mother, that it is not the custom with
us to sell a woman," he burst out. And his honest, kind
face flushed with anger. "She has a right to decide for
herself in such matters. What will become of respect-
ability, morality, and womanliness if such horrible prin-
ciples, which, alas ! are the order of the day, become
common ?· For my part, I despise a girl who marries
merely for the sake of a home ! " He stood before his
mother with sparkling eyes.

The old lady remained perfectly calm. Moritz had

always been a bit of an enthusiast, he got that from his father, and the "boy" did not know what life meant for an unprotected poor girl.

"Of course I cannot drag her to the church, and Hegebach is not the man to beg for a wife," was the reply. "What you say, my boy, sounds very pretty, if one possesses the necessary means. You know yourself that theory and practice are very different things. I have spoken on this subject often enough in these days. I shall say no more. I meant well. My grandmother used to say, 'Love—love is mostly imagination!' I have known plenty of girls who have been in despair at not being permitted to marry their first love, only to find afterward with the second that he was really the true, the only love. You are absurd, Moritz! Such views are only suited to a love-sick girl, or a half-cracked old maid."

"It may be," he replied roughly. "But I will not believe that many think as you do."

He had paused before Frieda and looked down at her with radiant eyes.

"Frieda, speak a word in honor of your sex."

"I do not know what she means." The little woman turned her beautiful head aside as if in embarrassment.

"Hegebach to-day asked for Elsa's hand, and she——"

"For Elsa?" the astonished eyes glanced from her husband to the busily knitting mother-in-law. "Indeed!" and she laughed loudly.

Involuntarily he started. What did this convulsive laugh, which was almost a sob, mean? Great tears were running down the pale cheeks.

"Of course you dissuaded her from accepting, Moritz," said she between her laughter.

"Dissuaded? No, Frieda; on the contrary, I tried to explain to her the necessity of this step, but I was nevertheless sorry to do so."

"Of course!" The young wife no longer laughed. "I could not imagine the castle without Elsa von Hegebach, it would be impossible."

"What do you mean by that?" interposed the old lady.

"Oh, nothing, dear mamma. Moritz surely understood me."

"Unfortunately no, Frieda," was the calm reply.

"But I do." Mrs. von Ratenow had risen, and now stood before her daughter-in-law. "I have been very considerate of you, my child, and of your whims and caprices, with which you tyrannize over the whole house, because I believed that you sincerely loved your husband. That he let you torment him was his affair; he wished nothing better. But when you dare"—she raised her voice loudly—"to accuse him, even in thought, of dishonor, when you dare to attack the reputation of the girl who has grown up under my roof—Frieda, by Heaven, I forget that you are the wife of my only son, the mother of his children!"

"Hush!" said Moritz, gently drawing down the old

lady's threateningly uplifted hand. " Frieda does not know what she is saying ; she means differently."

The young wife remained in her chair, pale as a corpse ; her face expressed a passionate defiance.

" No," she cried, springing up, " I do not mean differently ! I know what I have said. Since Elsa von Hegebach came to this house he has been a different man, he has eyes and attention for her alone ; I must certainly know it better than you and the others."

" Silence !" commanded the old lady so calmly and with such dignity that the beautiful mouth involuntarily closed. "What did I tell you, Moritz," she turned to her son, " when you courted your wife ? Do not weary of controlling her, or else she will get beyond control. Now you are reaping the harvest of your boundless indulgence, your foolishness. There are women and children for whom kindness is poison—and this was a love match ! Mine was not, but I *respected* your father and should never have dared to insult him. Now it is only necessary for you to beg her forgiveness, my boy, and the chapter of a modern conjugal romance is complete."

" You know very well, mother, that I shall not do that," he replied gloomily.

But the old lady only half heard it ; she had gone into her bedroom and bolted the door behind her.

" Frieda," said he sadly, turning toward her, " your imagination has misled you fearfully ; God knows you could not pain me more."

She still stood there pulling at her delicate handkerchief, her blue eyes shining with tears.

" Frieda, go back to your room and first grow calm," he pleaded, " then let us speak together quietly. My God ! how could you fancy such a thing ?"

He was pale ; she must see that she had wounded the great faithful man to the heart, but she would not see it. She shook off his hand and left the room hastily ; she was too deeply insulted, she was too unhappy a wife—oh——

" Lili," she sobbed in her boudoir, falling upon her sister's neck, " it is too terrible when, with all one's other misery, one has such a mother-in-law ! Old and big as Moritz is, he, nevertheless, is tied to her apron-strings like a child, and does not once take my part when she treats me like a school-girl. But why should he ? He loves me no longer ! "

It was a wretched day which neared its. close, and a wretched evening followed it. Frieda had shut herself into her room and would not see Moritz ; Lili told him this and looked at her brother-in-law as though he were a criminal of the worst kind. The children cried in their room, and when he wished to calm them they were frightened by his gloomy face. He then went out doors ; it was fairly suffocating in the house, he thought. Finally he walked down the driveway in the fragrant spring evening, and aimlessly strolled on through the city gate. The streets were very gay, the children played before the doors, and the neighbors gossiped

with each other, while the moonlight made it almost
bright as day.

"Hallo, my dear Ratenow!" cried a voice, and
some one tapped him on the shoulder. "What brings
you here? If you seek company, come to the Casino.
Rost is celebrating his betrothal."

Captain von P—— stood before him. Moritz was
not in the mood, he did not care to go; he excused
himself, saying he was not in evening dress, but finally
went.

In the elegant dining-room of the officers' club they
were very gay when the men entered. The happy
betrothed seemed the quietest of them all, except the
Bennewitzer who smoked his cigar apathetically.

"What the devil!" said Moritz, with difficulty taking
a jesting tone. "You here, Mr. von Hegebach? How
comes Saul among the prophets?"

"I was captured, as I suppose you were, dear Ratenow," he replied, drawing up a chair for Moritz. "I
did not care to drive home yet; you know, there are
days in life when one cannot rest."

Moritz was silent; he knew very well what that
meant, he himself had asked Hegebach early this morning to wait until to-morrow. Elsa was so surprised; his
offer had come upon her so suddenly; with everything
else which one is accustomed to say when a respite is
to be obtained.

They had already proceeded from punch to champagne; Rost was very lavish this evening, he had such

a "monstrously accommodating" future father-in-law, who, as he had told him to-day, would help him to settle up his debts ; a few bottles more or less of champagne could make no difference.

"Have you sent word to Bernardi, Rost ?" asked fat Assessor Dolling.

"Of course !" replied he. "I hope he will telegraph congratulations, for his letters are unendurable ; what he writes in his misanthropical mood is incredible !"

"His letters are better than himself," cried one of the young men ; "he does nothing but work or play on his violin. When I had leave recently I tried several times to bring him out a bit ; what is the use otherwise of being stationed in a half-way decent city ? But no, indeed. He remarked very condescendingly that such doings disgusted him, and that the Tivoli Theatre was to him simply horrible."

Most of the men laughed. "I troubled him no more," concluded the young officer, filling his glass. "Such a thing never worries us of the cavalry."

"I really believe that he will resign," remarked another very slowly, "for I learned accidentally that he asked my uncle, who is a kind of musical crank, whether he believed that his talent was sufficient to enable him to accomplish anything as a virtuoso, an artist."

"And I trust that your uncle said," interrupted the Assessor, imitating the speaker, "'Dear Bernardi, you are not very clever ; you are not a bad fiddler, but it takes more than that nowadays to become a virtuoso.'"

11

Lieutenant von Rost, who was not easily roused, suddenly changed color.

"Such a fellow!" he said softly to his neighbor on the left. "One has just with difficulty prevented him from committing an act of folly, and now he is about to commit a still greater one—he is simply crazy."

But his irritated remark was drowned by the noisy "*Hoch!*" which his comrades drank to the health of the young couple.

"Here's to Miss Annie Cramm! Let us drink to her health with three times three!" came from many animated voices.

"And a health to all beautiful women!" cried Captain von P——, and again the glasses clicked.

Moritz suddenly rose. It was not possible for him in his present frame of mind to remain here in this tumult.

"You are going?" asked the Bennewitzer. "I will come with you if you will permit."

"You are staying here in the hotel?" Moritz asked in the hall, while the enthusiastic toasts echoed from the dining-room.

"Yes! But I will accompany you, Ratenow."

It was now quiet on the street; only the moon bathed the city in its pale radiance, and a light mist hung over the roofs and wrapped the outlines of the houses and trees in a fairy-like veil. They walked on in silence, neither could find the right word to begin the conversation.

"My dear Ratenow," said the elder at length, "I do not want you, you especially, to judge me falsely. You looked at me so strangely a short time ago. I am neither vain enough to believe that a young girl like Elsa von Hegebach would rush with delight into my open arms, nor am I at the age when the expectation of the decisive word from a pair of red lips drives one hither and thither restlessly, and makes one, in case it is a refusal, think with satisfaction of suicide. I have borne too many hard blows of fate for that. The reasons which induce me to ask for my cousin's hand are only partly of an egotistical nature. My chief desire is that my cousin and his child may share our uncle's property, and this is the only way in which they can legally. But——" he stood still and laid his hand on his companion's shoulder. "I will add that I should not have formed this plan had not I conceived the greatest liking for the young girl. I say *liking*, dear Ratenow ; at my age one no longer speaks of passions."

They walked on. Moritz had continued silent, he knew so well that the man spoke the truth ; he knew that he could have chosen from many ; he was still a stately gentleman, a man with a noble, large heart, he might claim happiness, and yet——

"In the last weeks I have continually imagined how it might be, Ratenow," the Bennewitzer continued in a warm tone. "I have seen Elsa's figure gliding through my lonely rooms, and have heard her voice, so promis-

ing of happiness. I have gone to the room which I
destined for her father, and have planned the wedding
journey so as to show the wondering child's eyes the
other side of the Alps. God knows, Ratenow, it would
be an unspeakable pleasure to me to show this young
creature the thousand beauties with which nature and
man have adorned the world, and——"

He paused.

" I once crossed the Black Forest into Switzerland,
with my eldest boy, and I shall never forget the pleasure which I took in his unfeigned delight, his naïve
astonishment. I should like to see it again—Ratenow,"
he asked suddenly, "is not that some one ? "

They stood at the entrance to the carriage drive ; the
dark tree-trunks stood out distinctly in the moonlight,
and through the light mist, quickly, almost running,
a figure certainly did come toward them.

" It is a woman," said Moritz. "It is Elsa," he
added, after a minute. " Elsa, for God's sake, Elsa,
where are you going ? What do you want ? "

Suddenly she clung to him, he felt the trembling and
quivering of her body.

" Moritz, to father ! Take me to father ! "

" What has happened, Elsa ? Pray speak ! "

He loosed her arms from his neck and gazed at her
deathly-pale face.

" Ill," said she, with quivering lips. " Susan came,
she wished to summon me, then I ran away—take me
there, Moritz."

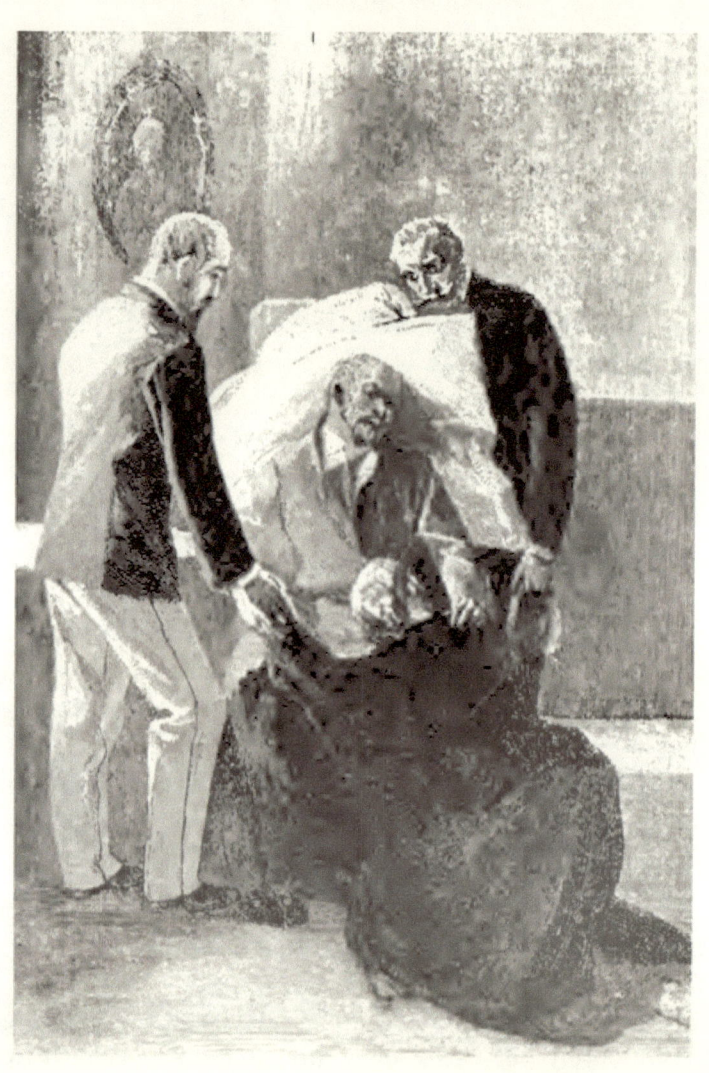

He drew her trembling hand within his arm. "Come, my girl."

"I will go with you," said the Bennewitzer. "Has a physician been sent for, do you know, Elsa?"

She shook her head and ran on, the men had difficulty in keeping up with her. She was without hat and coat, and in the uncertain light there was something uncanny in the way she flew on ahead. She had rushed up the stairs when the men reached the door. In the dim hall upstairs the physician came to meet them.

"Come in, gentlemen," he said softly. "I sent for his daughter—he will not live until morning."

They stood in the dingy sitting-room, the moonlight shone in brightly, and lay in a broad, white strip upon the floor, while the shadows of the young leafy twigs outside the window were reflected in it. "Tic-tac, tic-tac," said the old Black Forest clock, and through the half-opened door of the adjoining room came sounds like groans of pain.

"Papa!" cried a voice then, "do not go away from me, do not leave me so lonely, so fearfully lonely!"

The physician quickly took a step toward the door, then stood still again—the dying man spoke slowly, hesitatingly, and in disconnected, scarcely intelligible sentences.

"No, no, papa, do not die, do not die! I must tell you something, dear papa. Listen to me, can you hear me?"

The physician went in. After a moment he came

back and motioned to the Bennewitzer. He entered
the room, and his eyes sought the girl. She lay before
the chair in which her father rested, and embraced his
knees; the old man's right hand lay on her head, his
half-closed eyes were turned toward the entrance.

"It has come quickly, cousin, but I am much—
calmer than usual—because—Elsa, your hand. I have
done nothing for you in life, poor child, forgive me,
and you were always good and obedient—forgive me,
Elsa, make it easier for me to die—it was so hard—
life."

She raised her head and looked around as if begging
for mercy, but the weary eyes did not meet her gaze,
did not understand what she wanted. She only felt
that his hand with difficulty groped for hers, and when
he clasped it, made a weary effort to raise it and lay it
in another hand. All the sacred majesty of death
suddenly dawned upon her at sight of the fearfully
altered features, she gave herself up unresistingly to the
influence, then she felt a man's warm hand clasped
around hers, and that the dying man's right rested help-
lessly upon both.

"William, dear William," said a man's voice, with
emotion, "I will protect her and shield her—I promise
you!"

"Elsa!" whispered the dying man, "you will not be
left alone; no—poor—deserted girl—no, Elsa——"

She lay there without strength, her head on his knees,
her hand still clasped in the Bennewitzer's; it seemed

as though a blood-red mist rose before her eyes, and she could no longer think clearly. Then she heard Moritz's voice once more. "It is over. Come, Elsa, my dear child," and she felt some one raise her from the floor, then knew no more.

When she awoke to consciousness, Mrs. von Ratenow sat beside the sofa upon which they had put her to bed ; the old lady wore a wrapper, and had rested her head against the back of the chair and slept. The rays of the rising sun fell through the window, and filled the room with light.

The young girl started up abruptly, the scene of the night before rose to her mind suddenly as if by magic. Ah, it is terrible when a few hours of sleep have driven away sad remembrance; the weight of misery falls with double force upon the soul as it awakens, terrifying it anew, hurling it anew to the ground.

She drew her hand over her forehead. Was it all true ? And as if to convince herself, she rose and crept past the sleeping Mrs. von Ratenow into the adjoining room.

A draught of fresh air greeted her, the windows were opened, and a white cloth thrown over that which lay on the bed yonder. She stared at it immovably, her heart grew cold, and involuntarily she wrung her hands. "Our Father who art in Heaven—" flashed across her distracted mind ; she felt that she must pray, and yet had not the power to put her fear, her supplication into her own words—"and forgive us our debts as we forgive our debtors ! "

Then a startlingly shrill sound rang up into the room. Down in the street the trumpeter was blowing the usual reveille.

"His soldiers must wake up papa," Aunt Lott had once told the little girl when they had heard the gay sounds even in the castle.

"Come, Elsa, my dear child, that will never wake him again," said the voice of Mrs. von Ratenow; and she drew the girl to her breast. "It is well with him, my child, we must not grudge him his peace."

XII.

THE funeral was over. The gentlemen who had accompanied the body to the churchyard took leave at the gate of Moritz and the Bennewitzer.

Lieutenant von Rost crossed the road to greet his *fiancée* and her mother, who were taking a walk, perhaps not merely to breathe the fresh air, but also to see something of the funeral procession. Mrs. Cramm loved such things, and Annie no less ; a large fire, a wedding, or a funeral always attracted them to the scene.

The *fiancé* bowed and walked on beside Annie without offering her his arm. He was not of an especially chivalrous nature, and he had never spoiled his betrothed by too great attention, which Annie felt most painfully. It would have been so charming to walk along the streets together so tenderly and affectionately that every one might see how they loved each other.

"My dear son," began Mrs. Cramm, "have you heard how Miss von Hegebach is feeling now? She must be fairly petrified with grief, as Annie tells me."

The young lady nodded eagerly. "Yes, only think, Leo, I was there a short time ago ; she did not say a

word, and it was pitiful to see. She was not on such
deeply affectionate terms with the old man, and *au fond*
really has no cause for such despair. But she is fairly
crushed. Do you understand that ? "

He dropped his eye-glass. " Possibly," he replied,
"it is the result of two such shocks at once."

" 'Two ? " mother and daughter cried in the same
breath.

He was silent for a while, and then said, " She was
betrothed to the Bennewitzer beside her father's death-
bed."

A double cry of astonishment. " How lucky that girl
is ! " cried the round old lady in the black velvet cloak.

" It is astonishing, is it not ? " asked Lieutenant
von Rost, with an expression which made it doubtful
whether he spoke seriously or ironically.

" A great piece of good fortune ! " repeated Mrs.
Cramm. " That magnificent Bennewitz and the elegant
carriages ! Why, last year Prince H—— stayed there
for the hunting ! "

Annie was silent. She remembered how, when at
school, Elsa had often worn herself out over her books
studying for the governess's examinations ; how simply
she had always dressed. Yes, truly that was a piece
of good fortune. Who would have thought it ?

So the news of the betrothal of the so recently
orphaned girl to her cousin flew all over the city ; and
she herself sat in her little room in her long mourning
gown, her pale face rose ghostlike above the black

crape ruche, and her mouth wore an indescribably sad expression.

She had said but little since that morning, but Aunt Ratenow so much the more. She had not wept, but had gone about with a grief-stricken face, had moved from one spot to another, her hands in her lap, her eyes fixed gloomily upon the ground. She had taken scarcely any nourishment, had scarcely slept. She saw continually before her the discolored face of her dying father ; she felt the anxious groping for her hand, and how the chain closed around it, this invisible, horrible chain which she must wear for her whole life. Was it not more than horrible to avail oneself of the sacred power of the death-hour, the compelling force of a last wish, to make a human heart miserable for all life ? "Father, you did not love me," she groaned. And then again she saw the happy smile when he joined their hands ; the last, ah, so gentle breath, as though the poor breast were freed from a heavy weight. He died content, he died calm—and she must live, live ! It was horrible !

She had not yet seen him again, him in whose hand her father had placed her right hand ; and Mrs. von Ratenow had not urged this upon her. It was not compatible, this deep, silent grief, with betrothal happiness. But when they had returned from the burial, Mr. von Hegebach had asked to speak with her who had been intrusted to him in that solemn hour.

Mrs. von Ratenow, also in deep mourning, went up-

stairs to announce this important visit to Elsa. She
held a few twigs of cypress in her hand ; the Bennewitzer had taken them from the coffin before it was
lowered into the grave—a last greeting for the daughter.

The stately woman knocked less resolutely than
usual at the door, and then entered. Elsa sat beside
the table, writing materials lay before her ; she shut the
letter she was writing in the portfolio and rose. Mrs.
von Ratenow pressed the little cypress twigs into her
hand and stroked the pale cheek.

" Hegebach sends his love, he thought you would
like to drive with him to the grave, the carriage is
waiting, Elsa. Will you get ready ? He will come up
for you."

At the words " with him " she shuddered, and a deep
blush suffused her pale face for a moment. She did
not answer, but shook her blonde head slightly.

" Why have you drawn all the shades down ?" asked
the old lady, "as though God's sun were something
horrible," and she drew them up so that the glaring
sunlight streamed in and encircled the girl's head like
a halo. She closed her eyes, the rays were so piteously
bright.

" Look out-doors, Elsa." Mrs. von Ratenow took her
hand and drew her to the window. " See how the buds
are bursting on the apple-trees and how blue the sky
is ! One should honor the dead, child, but should not
forget the living for them, and you have duties in life ;
take heart."

The girl did not raise her eyes ; if possible, she grew paler.

"I am going down-stairs now, Elsa ; I have some-thing to say to Frieda. I will send your *fiancé* upstairs. At such times etiquette steps in the background, and besides he is no young idiot. When you come back from the church-yard you will take a cup of coffee with me. God bless you, Elsa ! "

She had gone. The girl clutched her forehead as though in agony, and the little hand clenched itself in her soft blonde hair. Was there no hope of escape ? Her eyes glanced around the room in horror ; now she was to fulfil a promise against which her whole heart rebelled. Ah, to be free, to be free once more ! It was horrible to know that all such thoughts were a sin. Mechanically she donned her dainty black mantle and bonnet. Then her hands dropped down limply, as she was about to fasten the strings—there on the threshold——

"Cousin," she stammered.

He came up to her and took both her hands in his ; now he drew them to his lips.

"My dear Elsa," said he gently, "it was a painful hour which brought us together, but also a grave and sacred one, the guarantee of a future of true, sincere happiness."

He spoke warmly, but nevertheless what he said sounded stiff, almost pedantic. It seemed as though the girl's chest rose as if relieved, but she was silent.

" Are you willing that we should now visit your father's grave together, Elsa ? "

She nodded. He took her parasol from the table,
handed it to her, and then offered her his arm. She

scarcely rested her hand upon it, and thus they left the
room, went down-stairs, through the hall and out to
the carriage. He helped her in, she seated herself on
the soft cushions of silver-gray silk, and he carefully

spread the handsome lap-robe over her knees. She had not once looked up ; now, as they drove quickly away, she glanced back. Mrs. von Ratenow stood in the window and waved her hand to them.

A feeling of indescribable misery came over the girl as she rolled away in the elegant carriage. It seemed to her that she had been sold, that she was unworthy of herself, and with a hasty gesture she drew the crape veil over her face. She was ashamed to let the bright clear spring sun shine into her eyes.

She did not notice his offered arm at the entrance of the church-yard ; she walked on hastily.

" Where are you going, Elsa ? " he asked. " The grave is on this side."

But already she had sunk down beside another mound, and was wringing her hands as though in despairing prayer. If she were still alive—a mother could never force her child into a loveless life, no, never !

He stood aside, calmly waiting. It was a long time before she rose, turned and followed him to the fresh grave on which the earth was still uneven—a sad sight which they had sought to conceal by numerous wreaths.

She stood here without a word, without a tear. He tried to take her hand, she drew it away from him gently.

" Shall we return ? " he asked after a quarter of an hour of deep silence. She assented and walked quickly on before him, down the narrow path between the rows of graves. At the carriage she hesitated. She would have much preferred walking. He silently offered her his hand to assist her to get into the carriage and seated himself beside her in silence. He knew what it was to return home from a fresh grave, he could easily understand her gloomy manner ; besides, she was always shy, grave, and somewhat cold. They would learn to laugh again, these brown childish eyes, when they need no longer look upon care and want, when the careless sunny existence in the comfortable rooms and beautiful park of Bennewitz had banished sad thoughts from the white brow. She would learn to smile again on their travels ; he would show her Paris first of all; she was only human, and Paris—Paris is an undefinably attractive word for a woman's ear.

She had covered her face with her veil again, and looked neither to the right nor the left. As they drove past the officers' club, Lieutenant von Rost and Captain von H—— stood in front of it. They bowed deeply, and looked after the carriage and the black veil which floated through the carriage window for a moment.

"She has not learned," said Rost, "to lie back among the cushions *à la grande dame ;* she sat up like a naughty child on a school-bench. Ah, well, it will not take her long ; women have a remarkable skill for such things."

"Do you think that she is in love with him ?" asked von H——.

"Bah !" said Rost, and turned toward his horse, which a groom just then led up.

XIII.

MEANWHILE Mrs. von Ratenow had been with Frieda. This young lady's temper had been as hopelessly bad as an equinoctial storm. She had scarcely a word of sympathy for the orphan. Lili had gone upstairs intending to be very cool in her condolences, but her good though flighty heart had gone out to the quiet, grief-stricken girl, and when she rejoined Frieda downstairs her eyes were red.

"Good gracious, why?" said the young wife crossly. "She has been very fortunate, I think. Pray do not go on like Moritz, as though a grand catastrophe had occurred."

"Why, Frieda, one does not look like that, in spite of all one's grief, when one is happily betrothed. No, Frieda, you are in a bad temper, and wish to have some one to be vexed with; I know you, little sister, eh? She has taken away one of your admirers, dear Frieda, eh? You cannot seriously be jealous of Moritz, good gracious! He has never cared for any one in all his life but just you."

But neither teasing nor reasoning had succeeded in

banishing the beautiful woman's bad temper; everything
had gone wrong since Elsa came here, and now there was
no prospect that she would leave the house.   One must
consider her mourning, she was no longer a nobody
who could be overlooked, she was betrothed to a man
who belonged to those who gave tone to his circle, who
was considered one of the leaders of society in the prov-
ince.   And Frieda fastened a coral brooch at the neck
of her dark-blue gown, for she would not participate
in the mourning.   What did she care about the surly
old man who had just closed his weary eyes?

But the old lady entered her daughter-in-law's room
with such an expression of satisfaction that the black
crape-trimmed gown was in strange contrast to her face.
All her hopes for the girl were about to be fulfilled, the
poor little thing had actually drawn the grand prize.
And how nicely she behaved, so grave, so reserved,
and yet so proud in her manners.   And how pretty she
looked in her deep mourning.   She had not once tried,
as before her father's death, to behave repellently and
roughly.   Ah, such a gaze into eyes which are about
to close forever has a grave, sacred power, and makes
everything which once had seemed important appear
mere trifles and childishness.   Elsa assuredly had gladly
grasped the protecting hand which was offered her just
at the moment when her little boat began to toss rud-
derless upon the wild sea of life.

"She is a good child, Elsa, God bless her!"   The
old lady did not mourn too deeply for the deceased.

She had indeed one regret, she would have been pleased had he been spared to live comfortably for a few years, but God knew best; they had never been very good friends, he and the Bennewitzer, perhaps he might have disturbed the perfect harmony. And he had always been an invalid—yes, yes, he was at peace—might he rest sweetly.

She sat down on one of Frieda's fragile arm-chairs, with a very pleasant "Good morning," and inquired after her little grandson's health in such a bright voice that the young wife's blue eyes rested upon her in astonishment.

"Well, Frieda, dear," she continued, with satisfaction, "what do you say to Elsa? Your late foolish fancies have flown, I trust." And she took Frieda's hand. "Listen, my child, a great load is taken off my mind; you can probably see it in my face, and when anything pleases me, you know that I like to see others pleased. You may wish for something particularly nice for your birthday, Frieda. Yes? Well, out with it, what will you have? Lili, help her."

The young wife's face did not yet clear, although what she had just heard sounded very promising; mamma Ratenow's gifts were always noble.

"You are very kind, dear mamma," came hesitatingly from the scarlet lips. "I——"

"Well you have time to think about it, do not hurry. How would it be if you and Moritz were to take a little trip, a season in Baden-Baden, then Switzerland and the Italian lakes—eh ? I will take care of the children. Well, think it over, my dear. Good morning. I will speak to Moritz about it. Good morning, children."

Ah, yes ; she knew how to find for every one the right tune to which she would willingly dance, and she also knew that she would never miss the effect she strove for. And so in this case. The two sisters suddenly sat close together on the lounge, and turned over the leaves of the newest fashion magazine ; here was such a pretty, stylish travelling costume if it were made up in different colors, say gendarme-blue. Moritz did not like to travel, it was too inconvenient and he dreaded the expense, for Madame Frieda did not travel cheaply, but now he could not help himself. Travel ! Oh, rapturous word ! Travel—Baden-Baden——!

Moritz was really the only one who continued obstinate.

"What is the matter with you, my boy ?" asked his mother. "How can you take Frieda's foolish jealousy so to heart ? She is on the best way to become sensible."

He put his hand to his head irritably. "You misjudge me, mother. I have simply ignored this fancy of Frieda's, although I cannot but admit that her behavior wounds me. It may be that she is partially right ; perhaps I was too prematurely anxious about the girl."

They walked across the yard together during this conversation. The spring sun bathed the old house in

a golden glow; the great linden at the gate had put out emerald-green, almost transparent leaves; on the roofs of the farm buildings, the doves sunned themselves in long rows, and suddenly soared up into the air, their wings resembling silver sparks against the deep-blue sky.

A carriage rolled quickly through the gateway, and stopped before the house door.

"The betrothed couple, Moritz," said Mrs. von Ratenow, walking more quickly. "Where are you going, Moritz?"

The son had taken his cap from his blonde head, and now turned toward the stable.

"I am going to look after Sultana; the veterinary surgeon is coming to-day to make another examination of her foot."

"Strange!" murmured the old lady, hurrying on, and she overtook the young pair just in the doorway, and pressed the girl's little black-gloved hand.

She looked strangely, Elsa, so rigid and determined. Good Heavens, her father—but this was unnatural; if she would but weep! And so she sat in the arm-chair in her aunt's comfortable room, drinking her coffee. The door into the garden-room was open, and the mild, soft spring air blew in on the stone paving of the terrace; the sun shone hotly, and a few rays fell in well-defined stripes on the floor, while myriads of atoms danced thereon.

The girl had turned her delicate head, and gazed into the next room immovably, with burning eyes, without speaking a word, without taking the slightest part in the conversation. Why should she?

She seemed to herself like one thrust out of a flowery garden into the ice and snow of winter; she shivered and seemed frozen, frozen to the very marrow of her bones. And from beyond, blooming roses nodded to her and asked : "Why do you let them urge you to this?"

And the swallows flew by, chirping : "Is this your courage? Are you not ashamed?"

And she was ashamed, so ashamed that she sprang up and hurried out onto the terrace and down into the garden, through the dear old paths, with flying feet.

"My dear Mrs. von Ratenow," said the Bennewitzer, when Elsa left the garden-room so suddenly, "is my betrothed ill? I must tell you frankly that this silent despair worries me. Is it really the shock at the sudden death *alone* which has so wholly changed her?"

The old lady shook her head carelessly.

"My dear Hegebach! The girls of the present time are different from those of our day. Then they were fresh, healthy creatures ; to-day a bit of misanthropy is a part of good tone. And, besides, remember it is the day of the funeral, and in spite of everything she loved her father absurdly, tenderly."

"Do you think so?" he asked slowly, settling himself more comfortably in his arm-chair than he had permitted himself in the young girl's presence. "I do not know. It was principally the expression of the eyes. When I went to her room this afternoon she gave me a look—yes, you will call me sentimental, my dear madame, but I cannot forget this look, it was so reproachful, questioning. A pair of eyes looked at me thus once before, and I could never forget it. It was in Russia ; a young gypsy woman stood by the roadside and begged. My coachman, a rough fellow, gave her a cut over the head with his whip. She did not move an eyelash, but her large dark eyes turned to me ; a world of misery lay in this glance. And a mouth drawn with pain. Those eyes, those questioning, reproachful eyes, were Elsa's when I entered her room to-day. And I— I cannot help it, I must say it—there is more in them than grief for her lost father."

"Hegebach !" came in a tone of the deepest reproof. A very strange feeling overcame the stately woman, at his words. She shook her head and looked at him closely, but she did not know what reply to make. In her embarrassment she picked up the coffee-pot and filled her cup to the brim ; she rose, presented her guest with a cigar, and asked : "Where can Elsa be ? Shall we take a walk in the garden ?"

They wandered down various paths, but did not discover Elsa. Frieda and Lili returned with the children from a walk ; they looked over the wall and saw Moritz riding off. He bowed to them and cried that he was going to inspect the fields.

"I do not understand where Elsa can be ; she is a strange girl." And "Elsa, Elsa !" echoed all over the garden, in the lady's strong voice.

All was silence.

"Pray, dearest Mrs. von Ratenow, leave my *fiancée* in peace. She seems not inclined to talk, and I can feel for her."

They walked on in silence. Here and there he stopped and looked at a budding twig and gave the botanical name. The excited woman at his side did not answer.

"I must take leave early to-day." The Bennewitzer paused and drew out his watch. "Pray give Elsa my warmest love."

"I will have her looked for, dear Hegebach."

"No, pray do not ; perhaps she is crying her grief out. Do not disturb her, my dear madam ; I will come again to-morrow. One must never force a liking."

He called to the gardener who just then passed, to order his carriage, calmly continued smoking his cigar, and spoke of a few very foreign matters.

"Apropos, dear Hegebach," the old lady interrupted, "what did you say was the name of the Berlin jeweler of whom you ordered the engagement ring ?"

"Haller & Company," he replied. "It will not be finished before a week."

"Of course not," she remarked, "because there is always a rush of such business. Thomas, here on Market street, could have attended to it just as well and quicker. But you are like all the rest, Hegebach."

He smiled but did not answer.

"I believe the carriage drove by," he then said. "Permit me to take leave of you now, until to-morrow, Mrs. von Ratenow; and greet my sad little Elsa for me."

He kissed her hand, mounted the terrace steps elastically and disappeared into the house. After a while his carriage rolled rapidly over the paved yard.

"Of course he is vexed," said Mrs. von Ratenow, who still stood at the foot of the veranda steps. "The child behaves inexcusably. Good Heavens, how provoking young people are! She should have been my father's daughter," and she turned and walked up and down the garden path again, with great strides and a very excited face. Very well, she would say nothing more to-day, but to-morrow—it was unheard-of to run away so stupidly, and it was even dangerous.

"And what does that mean that the Bennewitzer told me, that story about her eyes? Merely that at his age he yet stares at the child like a boyish lover, the softhearted fellow; he was not like that formerly," and she drew her hand over her forehead and for a moment stood still in the dairy, like a ghost, so that the maid almost fell on her knees in alarm; she had thought her mistress anywhere but here; surely she was upstairs drinking coffee with the engaged couple.

"Well, pray do not swoon," she said in her loud voice. "It is the fashion now;" and she went from pan to pan, and looked into all the butter-tubs. She was in a bad temper, the mistress. She could not even knit

as usual ; she saw continually before her the girl's pale
face, and heard the Bennewitzer talk of her eyes. She
could not help it, she must speak with her—in all kindness, but speak with her she must.

She rose to go upstairs ; then Moritz came and seated
himself in his father's easy-chair opposite her, and he
had all sorts of matters to discuss with her. His question: "Has Hegebach gone already ?" she answered
with a short: "As you see,' and then hurriedly turned
the conversation to the state of the crops ; she could
not tell him how the girl behaved.

"Where is Elsa ?" he asked.

"Probably upstairs. But how did you happen to
have Sultana treated by the young veterinary ? I saw
him go into the stable a short time ago."

"I did not want my favorite to wait long, and the
older man is ill."

"Oh, indeed," said she, but she was thinking of
something quite different. And then the young ladies
and children came in. Lili was so gay and the children
so droll, they had a merry time in the twilight hour.
When the children at length said good-night it was
quite late, and the moon shone brightly upon the roofs
of the out-buildings.

"Will you take tea with us ?" asked Moritz, "and is
Elsa coming down-stairs ?"

"Thank you, no," she replied; "Sophie may bring
our tea here ; Elsa is not in the mood, you know."

"Then, good-night, mother ! "

The old lady rose quickly from her chair ; she must speak with Elsa.   She went upstairs hurriedly and opened the door of the girl's room ; it was filled with white light, the windows were wide open, and with the moonlight had crept in a sweet perfume of violets. It was perfectly silent in the room ; nothing stirred.

"Elsa," she called softly, and looked around the room.   There lay the girl on the bed ; the old lady went up to her and bent over her.   Really, she slept ! And in her hand she held a little bunch of faded violets pressed closely to her breast.   But at the foot of the bed stood the old chest, and half out of it hung a crumpled white gown.

She knew both gown and. bunch of violets, and in her mind she saw the girl before her as she had looked that evening of the dance, with her happy child's eyes.   The old lady stood there motionless, she suddenly felt so strangely, felt as she had not for long years.   Was this caused by the perfume of the violets and the long-drawn sweet tones of the nightingales floating up from the garden outside ?   She crept out into the corridor on tip-toes, and then she stood in her dark room, her hand pressed to her forehead, motionless, for a long time.

"Nonsense," said she at length, in an undertone, and went to the little table where she kept the matches. And "Nonsense," she repeated again loudly, as she struck a light.   "To-morrow morning I will give her a good talking-to."

XIV.

VERY early in the morning rain had fallen, and the rising sun was hidden by dark clouds, but how green and fresh was the earth!

The maids were busy in the kitchen, the men were beginning to feed the cattle, but for the rest the whole house was still, except for a light step which came along the corridor and down the stairs; through the lower hall and kitchen it hurried, and out into the open air.

It was very cool, and Elsa von Hegebach drew her veil over her face as she crossed the yard and went out through the gate. The housekeeper, about to enter the dairy, looked after her, shaking her head.

"I think she must be going to the churchyard," said she to the cook.

" She had a travelling bag in her hand," said another, and then they went about their work.

In the stable-door stood a tall, blonde man, and his honest blue eyes followed her gravely. He knew what she was about to do, and he did not move a foot to hurry after her, to detain her. " But where is she going?" he asked in an undertone; and so he stood motionless until the dark figure had vanished at the end of the

driveway. Then he examined his sick horse again, stroked her shining neck, as she looked at him with her intelligent eyes, and when, a half hour later, he slowly crossed the yard to the house, he heard the shrill whistle of a locomotive from the other side of the city.

"Farewell, Elsa, my poor girl," said he softly. "I do not know whether you have done wisely, but that you have done rightly I am sure."

It was about nine o'clock when Mrs. von Ratenow sent her maid upstairs to ask Miss von Hegebach to come to her. The old lady sat by the window as usual, looking very grave and a trifle pale. She had had a bad night; oppressive dreams with all kinds of evil forebodings had troubled her. The fatal white gown and withered violets, and the girl's strange manner yesterday had played a great part in them. And to-day, by sober daylight, the old lady had become furious with herself; she should have waked the girl yesterday evening, have scolded her, and told her that as a bethrothed she should not think of the other.

And who was this other? A young fellow like dozens of others, distinguished by nothing but a bit of talent for violin-playing. She must put an end to it, kindly, but still must put an end to it.

"The young lady is not in her room," reported the maid.

"Look in the garden!" was the command.

"Oh, mercy!" The servant stood still. "I do not believe the young lady is there, ma'am. The housekeeper says that Miss von Hegebach went to the church-yard almost before day this morning."

"Nonsense!" The old lady rose. "When was that?"

"About four o'clock, madam, the housekeeper says."

"And now it is nine! Look in the garden."

The girl went. Her mistress seated herself calmly in her chair again, and stared out across the yard. The maid did not come. The old lady *would* not worry. Where could Elsa be? She would surely come soon.

"I cannot find Miss von Hegebach," said the servant. "Dora says she had a bag in her hand."

"Very well, she will soon come——"

The girl left the room. For a while, the old lady remained at her post, then went upstairs to the missing girl's room. All as usual—nothing was gone but the little portfolio, the crucifix over the bed, and her prayer-book, but as yet she did not notice that. The chest was carefully closed, and when Mrs. von Ratenow raised the lid, there lay the crumpled white gown, carefully folded. "She is coming back again. God knows what she intended doing this morning early."

Then she went up to the little table under the book-shelves, again; there lay a letter. "A letter—sealed?" And in a such a scratchy, new-fashioned hand-writing. The old lady must first put on her spectacles. "Mrs. von Ratenow," she read.

She seated herself and broke the seal, slowly, very slowly, but she had grown white to the lips.

"Dear, dear Aunt:

"Do not think me too unthankful because I secretly leave your house in which I have been so very kindly treated all my life. No choice remained for me. I stood weaponless and weary, in opposition to you all. I found only sufficient strength—to go. I cannot live with a lie in my heart. I could not bring my lips to utter the truth. I wished to yesterday, when I stood with Mr. von Hegebach beside papa's grave—and I could not speak a word. I do not know whether you understand me, aunt. I pray to God that you will judge me mildly.

"I will write to Mr. von Hegebach from D——, where I am going. I know that he is too noble not willingly to give me back the promise which was forced from me in a moment of paralyzed will and when I was half fainting with fear.

"Good-by, dear aunt. I am and remain always in sincere thankfulness,

'Your deeply grateful niece.

"Elizabeth von Hegebach."

"P. S.—I can easily obtain a position of assistant-teacher in D——. Do not worry yourself about my future."

The trembling hands dropped the letter. "Good Heavens!—how was it possible?"

Once more she raised the letter to her eyes as though she could not have read it correctly, then looked at her watch, and rising went to her room as though bowed by a heavy weight. She rang the bell, and with averted face, ordered the maid, "Ask my son to come here."

"The Baron has gone out riding," was the answer.

She went into her bed-room and began to gather together all things necessary for a journey. But she always took up the wrong articles, frequently put her hand to her head; finally she consulted the time-table. The train to Halle left at eleven o'clock.

She rang once more and ordered the carriage, and directed that John was to take a note to the Bennewitzer at once.

" Mr. von Hegebach is in the city ; I saw his carriage this morning," remarked the girl, timidly.

Had everything gone wrong this morning ?   " Very well," said she again, but her anger began to rise.   This was the thanks for all her kindness !   Elsa ran away like a romance heroine ; in her boundless thoughtlessness she thrust from her all that through most unlooked-for good fortune, had fallen to the lot of her, the homeless one ; she compromised herself and the house in which she had found a home.   The gentle girl with the mild brown eyes, where had she gotten this unfortunate energy ? But she must not yield to her ; the letter to the Benne-witzer must be prevented at any price.

She went to her secretary and wrote a telegram to the principal of the institute at D——, telling her to persuade Elsa not to write a line before she had had an interview with her ; she would come by the night train, and begged hospitality.   She sent one servant with the sealed dispatch, and wrote to the Bennewitzer—he must be found in the hotel, the court-house or the club—that he must not come here to-day.   They would be forced to deceive him as to the reason, but how hard it was with this honest, sincere nature.   She tore the third sheet. Elsa had a headache, she had thought of writing first, but he would surely learn that she had gone out. She had been forced to leave home suddenly—Pah! where could she have gone? He would at once know that all was not in order. No, she could not lie. Come what would, she saw no help for it.

"If Moritz were only here!"

"A messenger from Mr. von Hegebach." The girl brought a bouquet of May-flowers for Miss von Hegebach, and a note to Mrs. von Ratenow.

"Carry the bouquet to Miss von Hegebach's room," she commanded, and then broke the seal of the note.

It ran as follows :

"My intention, my dear madam, to dine with you to-day has unfortunately become impossible to fulfil. I must at once return to Bennewitz, as I expect the building commissioners of the M—— Railway, which is to cross my land. Forgive my haste. I hope to be able to pass a few hours with you and my *fiancée* to-morrow in your pleasant home.

"Sincerely yours,

"HERMANN VON HEGEBACH."

"Thank God, a respite is won!" Mrs. von Ratenow's courage rose again. She could take the eleven o'clock train; she could surely count upon sister Beata's assistance. The girl must not thus trample upon her happiness. She continued her preparations. Good heavens, what she had to do for this defiant girl! How she hated railway travelling; and she must change cars in Halle. Ah, and the horrible confusion in Halle. Suddenly a new idea occurred to her; she had heard the

13

sound of a horse's hoofs, and went to the window. Truly, it was he.

"Moritz!" she called loudly.

He bowed and smiled. "Immediately, mother."

He attended to all kinds of business first; she heard him speaking to the gardener in the hall; at length he appeared.

"Good heavens, my boy, how slow you are!" said she, irritably.

"Were you in a hurry, dear mother?"

"It is a quarter past ten, Moritz, and—will you do me a favor, Moritz? You know how I hate to travel— you go to D——, speak to Elsa; she always thought the most of you. You know nothing as yet, Moritz; do not know that the girl has run away. Or—yes! Moritz, did you know anything of it?" She looked at him closely.

He remained so calm in spite of her hasty words.

"Yes, mother, I saw her go away."

"Moritz! And you did not prevent her, did not try with all your might to dissuade her from her crazy, sentimental idea?"

There he stood, so large and broad-shouldered.

"No, mother!" And he picked up his riding-whip from the table, and twisted it in his hands, as defiantly as when he was a boy, when things went contrary to his wishes. "No, mother. I had no right to do so."

"Good heavens, Moritz!" The old lady had become crimson with rage.

"No right!" he repeated. "Neither I nor you, mother; no one has the right, thank God, by our laws to force a girl to marry against her will."

"It is simply maddening! What fine speeches are these! Who forced her decision in the final moment?"

"Every one and everything! People, circumstances, life and death, mother. And her own heart cried 'No!' But no one would hear it."

"But why, Moritz? Can you not see the reason? Is it not madness in her position?"

"Reason? Yes. Do not ask, mother. Who has ever fathomed the mystery which attracts a heart to one and turns it from another?"

"You speak like a romance writer, Moritz. Pray look about the world. It is day, bright day; human life is prosaic, no idyll; it is a struggle and conflict, and each person must look out for himself."

"And what turns the wheels is love, mother; and love will not be driven from the world, however the realists may try. Love and fidelity—they are in the blood of us Germans, mother." He nodded gravely. "I cannot explain it to you, it requires finer words than I have at my command."

"Love?" The old lady burst out. "Love?" she repeated. "You mean the little Lieutenant. What is he in comparison to the Bennewitzer? A nobody, a good-for-nothing; he has drawing-room manners and can play the violin a little—*voilà tout.*"

"I merely know that he is an agreeable man," per-

sisted Moritz. " But nevertheless this is a mystery.
Love does not ask for outward things, for position,
charms; and then—a good-for-nothing, mother ? Confess frankly that if Bernardi were, well say for example,
the Bennewitzer's son, how then ? "

" Then it would be quite different, my boy. Cease
your sentimental nonsense. Will you go ? " she asked,
dictatorially. " Will you once more speak to Elsa, lay
the whole matter before her ? For — absurd — she
certainly can not marry her Bernardi. He has probably
long ago forgotten her besides."

" In one thing I admit that you are right, mother—
he cannot marry her at present. I do not know
whether he has forgotten her, but do not believe so, for
this morning Rost's valet brought, in Bernardi's name,
a beautiful wreath for the grave. But as to going after
Elsa—no, mother. I have just given you my opinion,
I shall not persuade the child."

" Good ; then I go ! "

" Do not, mother dear ; it is not right."

" Shall she reproach me later when she has become a
nervous old governess ? " she asked. " I shall do my
duty ! "

" It is useless, mother, especially now, in her fearful
excitement."

" God helps those who help themselves ! " said she.
" You are the same old enthusiast ! " And she went into
her bedroom.

XV.

THE express train whirled her along the same road
over which she had travelled before, but then it was an
autumn foggy evening, and her heart had been full of
happy expectation ; now it was a spring morning, and
the sun shone in the carriage window so pitilessly, ex-
posing every spot and hole in the shabby cushions.
The little mirror opposite reflected a pale face with a
weary expression about the mouth ; and this was she,
Elsa von Hegebach. She leaned back against the
cushion exhausted, her eyes gazing unchangedly at the
flying landscape. She did not see that the world basked
in all the splendor of spring, her young heart was so
terribly gloomy and empty.

Now she had burned her bridges behind her; now she
had no one who understood her, no one ! Even Aunt
Lott had written in a strange half-sentimental, half-
jubilant tone, that it was a great happiness which had

fallen to her lot, an enviable happiness to have drawn such a prize. Happiness! People called that, happiness! And what? To bear the name of a man, to share his wealth, to have no care for the thousand material needs of life—that was their happiness! And for that she must give up everything, her liberty, her thoughts, her hopes, even herself, body and soul! A nervous shudder overcame her; she closed her eyes. "Never!" said she, so loudly that she started at the sound of her own voice, and the old lady opposite her looked at her in astonishment.

She lowered her lashes without noticing it; she saw only a dark red glow before her eyes, and in this glow, nearing and then fading away as soon as she tried to see it plainly, a dark curly-haired man's head, with melancholy eyes and a little black moustache. Above the noise of the train, she seemed to hear sleigh-bells, and inhale the perfume of violets. And yet he had turned from her, had deserted her—because she was a poor girl!

She started suddenly.

"Dear child, are you ill?" asked a sympathetic voice, and an old woman's face was bent over her.

"No, no!" said she hastily, flushing deeply. "But I did not sleep last night, and——"

"Pardon me; you groaned so, my dear young lady." The lady seated herself again and opened a sachel in which lay a number of little bunches of violets. "My grandchildren picked them for me; may I offer you one?" And she held out the sweet flowers to the girl.

The little hand grasped them, but she uttered no thanks. The giver merely saw that she hastily drew her black veil over her face, and beneath that, pressed the flowers to her lips ; after a while she thought she heard sobs, but such strange sobs, as though one were weeping with dry eyes. "Already unhappiness, and she is so young," she whispered, and looked out of the window.

All was change on the railway ; at times the carriage was full for a short distance, then it was empty again. And now the old lady left the train. She stood on the station platform, and gazed after it as it slowly rolled away. She would have liked to see the sad childish face again ; in vain, she sat as motionless among the cushions as ever.

And now slowly, slowly Elsa reached her destination. She stood on the platform of the well-known station ; it seemed to her as though she were dreaming. The blue Thuringian mountains rose in the distance, as she had seen them a hundred times. Ah, the beautiful forest, the great, broad, solitary forest, how happy she had been when she walked through it ! And here it lay before her, the village with its scrupulously clean streets. the neat old houses in which behind every window bloomed flowers ; down there the plain little church, and near by the shady green churchyard. All so unchanged ; only she—only she !

Hastily she walked on down the street, past the long fence and through the garden. Not a soul to be seen—thank fortune! They were all at work in the school-room as yet. The narrow, dazzlingly white stairs creaked softly as the girl ascended. How natural that sounded! She knew this creak so well. And hark! Then she heard the canary-bird singing in Sister Beata's room.

She knocked and slowly crossed the threshold of the little room in her mourning clothes, with the gloomy veil over her pale face.

"Elizabeth!" said a deep, calm voice. "Is it really you, Elizabeth?"

And a little old woman in the dress of the Moravian Sisterhood came up to her, a pair of indescribably mild eyes gazed into her grief-stricken face.

"Sister Beata," she tried to say, but she could not; she merely threw both arms around the old woman's neck, and all the torment of the past few days found vent in convulsive weeping.

"You are in mourning, poor child?"

"My papa—" she stammered.

The little sister pressed her hand gently and led her to an old-fashioned sofa. "First calm yourself, Elizabeth; we will talk later. Come, take a cup of coffee. I knew that you were coming—a despatch has arrived."

"From whom?" The girl looked at the speaker in horror. "What do they want? What does the telegram say?" she added hastily.

"I must prevent you from writing a letter, child, and then—your aunt will arrive this evening."

Elsa sat there silent and trembling. "She will not let me!" she sobbed at length. "Sister Beata, help me from sinning as only a girl can sin ; save me from ruin !"

"Elizabeth, you are beside yourself," said the sister's calm voice reprovingly.

Elsa was silent, and the hands which involuntarily she had clasped sank in her lap. She gazed gloomily and with close scrutiny at the passionless face before her.

"Sister Beata," she began, in a totally changed voice, "you told me when we parted that I could always find refuge with you ; that you could always give me employment in your school. I come to-day to ask you for it."

"It is most opportune, dear Elizabeth. The place of Sister Angelica in the fourth class is free."

With these words the speaker held out a plate of inviting looking cake to the young girl.

She declined it, however. "Where is Sister Angelica ?" she asked.

"She has gone to Africa. Elizabeth, you should eat; you look so exhausted."

"To Africa ? As a missionary, I suppose ?"

"Yes ; she will assist her husband, who has a school in Natal. The lot fell to her, and so she has gone ; she left three weeks ago."

It sounded so calmly, it was said so simply, as though Sister Angelica had driven to a neighboring town. Elsa knew her well, the delicate blonde girl; and she also knew that the society was accustomed to marry its daughters by lot. She had never thought of it; now it seemed to her something unworthy of human beings.

"And she was willing to go, Sister Beata?" she asked, and clasped her throbbing temples.

"Willing? That, she probably confided to God alone, but she knows that it is His will; she went joyfully."

All was silent in the little room. The air seemed oppressively close, to the young girl. Sister Beata now sat by the table before the window, correcting exercises. "You should rest awhile, Elizabeth; you look pale and exhausted," said she. The girl shook her head, and going up to her laid her hand on her shoulder.

"Sister Beata," she began, in a trembling voice, "you told me once—not so very long time ago—that truth is the only thing that can save us from need and distress; that it stands above all other virtues."

The little head under the snowy-white cap nodded assent, without looking up. "Certainly, dear Elizabeth; you were always an honest, good child as far as human intelligence could judge."

"What I am about to ask you sounds strangely, Sister Beata, but Angelica wore no other image imprinted upon her heart; she did not stand before the altar with a lie on her lips?"

Now she looked up, the quiet sister. "No, Elizabeth;

her heart was like an unwritten page. We live a quiet and secluded life here; the passions which torment and pain foolish human hearts out in the world do not cross our threshold, we scarcely know them from hearsay. You must know that, Elizabeth. What do you mean by your question?"

The girl suddenly fell on her knees before her, and buried her head in the folds of the gray woollen gown.

"I wish I had never gone away from here; I wish I had never seen him!" she sobbed.

"Stand up, Elizabeth, and control yourself."

The sister stroked the girl's hair compassionately.

"Help me, Sister Beata," pleaded Elsa, looking at her with tearful eyes; "help me not to be wicked and deceitful! Tell my aunt that I must write and tell him the truth at any price."

"Him—Elizabeth?"

"Yes; him to whom I have been betrothed for three days."

Sister Beata made no reply.

"You have always been my favorite, Elizabeth," said she, after a moment, "but will you be content here? Do not think it so easy after having been out in the gay world, to settle down here as a teacher, to have nothing but duty before your eyes and the hand of the clock which points to the hour for work. Once, years ago, a dear scholar came back, weary of the world, sick at heart, and asked for work, begging me to keep her always, always. At first all went excellently;

she worked to forget her sad thoughts, the quiet and regularity did her distracted nerves good. Then time healed the wounded heart, and health came and allured her back to the fresh, happy, outer life ; her gaze became more and more longing, and one day she said, ' I am going, Sister Beata ; I must go. Here one creeps ; out in the world one flies ! ' And she went. I do not know what has become of her. I only tell you this to make it clear to you that this is no place to heal wounds which the world has inflicted. If you accept the position, Elsa, you pledge yourself for two years at least. Consider that well."

She still lay on her knees, and wild thoughts whirled through her brain. Airy garments danced before her eyes, red roses and floating scarfs ; she heard gay music, laughing and singing—that was life, that was youth. And, like a colorless picture, she suddenly saw the school-room before her, with its bare wall ; gray, monotonous gray was the life here, and she was so young ! The sister's last words weighed like lead upon her heart.

Hark ! From the adjoining room a sound rang out in the silence, clear and vibrating : a violin was being played in there. A violin ! Suddenly she sobbed again, and pressed her blonde head down on her crossed arms, which still rested on the old woman's lap. Those were the thorns of the crimson roses, the painful thorns !

" I have nothing more outside ; nothing more, Sister Beata ! " she stammered. " I will stay with you."

XVI.

THERE were spare rooms in the school. The hotel of the little town was very primitive, and occasionally a mother wished to stop over in passing through, to visit a daughter. A room had been opened for Elsa, and the best of these modest apartments arranged for Mrs. von Ratenow.

The train would arrive at nine o'clock; and the principal had gone to the station, herself, to receive the stern aunt. Meanwhile Elsa sat in her room, and with increasing dread gazed at the driving clouds, which now covered the moon, now exposed her round full face, for which teasing play she outlined them with silver. What would happen now? Sister Beata had at length learned all the details of her story, and told herself that the poor child had had no choice. She was sufficiently acquainted with Mrs. von Ratenow, from her decided letters, to know that there would be a harder conflict yet.

According to Elsa's calculation they must have been back from the station for some time already. Now the two who held the threads of her destiny in their hands were surely sitting in the cosey sitting-room, fighting for her so-called happiness.

"Elsa! Elsa!" cried a soft voice. "Are you here or not?"

She started, and her eyes, accustomed to the darkness, perceived the slight girlish figure in the door, and recognized the coquettish spring hat, and the small aristocratic face beneath.

"Lili?" she asked in surprise.

"Yes, it is I!" was the answer. "I imagined that I would find you just this way, looking at the moon, of course!

> 'Moon, thou art happier than I,
> Thou seest him, and I see him not!'"

she continued, tearing off her hat. "Good gracious, is there not a sofa here? I am frightfully tired. Oh, Elsa, this was a wild idea of yours to run away!"

"You accompanied Aunt Ratenow, Lili. She—she is here?"

"Why, of course!" And the dainty figure threw itself on the white bed and stretched to her heart's content. "She would have been sitting in all her glory in Halle had it not been for me. Moritz knew that very well, or else he would surely have spared me this journey. The whole compartment full of mothers, nurses and babies, and among them all, stiff as an Indian pagoda, Aunt, on the hunt for you, and I—Oh, Elsa, why did you inflict this upon me? This evening there is a supper at the Cramms', and I am so fond of stewed crabs and asparagus ! "

Elsa did not answer ; she silently seated herself beside the bed upon which Lili rested and gazed, anxiously in her face, from which, in spite of her complaints, the eyes shone with an expression of the utmost satisfaction.

" Listen, Elsa ; you have furnished excellent matter for gossip in the city," continued the little lady. " I must confess that when Moritz brought the alarming news this morning, and also the order for me to accompany Aunt on her pursuit of the fugitive, I had no greater desire than to dine at the officers' mess to-day. I am convinced that the bar-tender will do a flourishing business, in the excitement. One glass after another will be emptied. And Rost will surely have drawn you, probably as a nun behind a lattice, and the Bennewitzer kneeling before it, with clasped hands, with plumed hat and sword, and beneath written : 'Knight, this heart devotes itself to you in a true sisterly love. ' It is really very modern, the mediæval German. But I should like to know how you happened to think of this, sweet child ? "

She received no answer. Elsa stood at the window again.

" I do not understand you," continued the little chatterbox. " I find the Bennewitzer wonderfully *chic* to marry. I assure you if he had wished me—*au moment!* although I also cherish a so-called love, here." She pointed to her heart. " One must have some one to think of, you know, Elsa, when one reads poems, for instance Geibel or Strachwitz. For that, it is highly necessary, but nevertheless I would have married the Bennewitzer. How charming for *him* to see me again chained to another ; he must feel quite like Heine. '*Ewigverlornes Lieb—ich grolle nicht!* ' One need not be miserable long, that is only for poets ; but it is interesting, highly interesting, Elsa ! Elsa, do not be angry with me," the girl suddenly whispered coaxingly, and two soft arms were thrown round Elsa's neck. " I am not as bad as I seem, and if you will promise me not to cry any more—do you think I do not see that you have been crying ? I tell you, you have cried your dear eyes, red—why, then I will tell you something that will please you mightily."

" Nothing will please me now, Lili," was the sad answer, as she leaned her forehead against the window panes.

" I have seen *him*, Elsa," was whispered still more softly, " as large as life and twice as natural ! "

" My—my cousin ? " groaned the tortured girl. It was horrible for her to be forced to hear how he had received this blow from her hand. She saw him so plainly before her, as he had stood beside her at her father's grave, and looked at her so kindly, so compassionately. Even then she had raised her hand for this blow, but it had sunk down powerless.

" The Bennewitzer ? The poor cast-off Bennewitzer ? I do not mean him," continued Lili, leaning closer against the trembling form. "We girls call only one, the very particular one, *him*. Nonsense, Elsa, do not be so childish ; you are nineteen years old, and were at boarding-school. Oh, yes," she interrupted herself with a laugh, "with the Moravians ; I forgot. One never learns anything with them, their boarding-school girls are pure, unsophisticated angels at eighteen years old, I suppose. I was at G——, and from our school-room we could look out upon the parade-ground, and every one of us called some one down there, *him*. Well then, I saw *him* in Halle—Elsa, do you understand ? He had his violin-case in his hand, and wore civilian clothes, and—well, not exactly of the latest style, but with the military we close one eye at that ; it is more practical in a large city ; for instance, he could drive an omnibus in such clothes without attracting attention through their elegance. Well, Elsa, what do you say ?"

Elsa did not move.

"And I spoke to him—do not start so, Elsa. Aunt did not see it. She was conferring with the porter on the other side of the platform. I bought the tickets—there he stood in the crowd. He is handsome, Elsa, really. I knew him too slightly to address him, had only danced with him once, but—I know how to manage ! Crash ! my umbrella lay at his feet as I passed. Of course he picked it up. 'Oh, thank you a thousand times, Lieutenant Bernardi !' He started. 'I am in a great hurry,' said I, mentioning my name, Lili Tees-feld. 'I am going with Aunt Ratenow to D——, to

14

catch Elsa Hegebach ; she absolutely wishes to go into
a cloister ! ' You should have seen his face. ' Yes, yes,
into a cloister,' I nodded, ' because she will not marry
her cousin. Good-by, Lieutenant Bernardi ! ' I left
him standing, and courageously forced my way through
the crowd, but just as I was about to get into the ladies'

compartment, he stood beside our train, and got into
the next carriage. Fortunately, Aunt sat at the window
on the opposite side. I needed air very often, so did
he, especially at the stations. Meanwhile, Aunt interrupted her conversations with the nurses, ' Are you talking to any one, Lili ? ' Whereupon I—oh, well, I can

look surprised, I assure you. In short he knows all, and I am to be good, very good to you. He said that, as I got out. He went on in the train. And when I tell you that he sent a wreath for your papa's grave, and that he is now going home on leave, I have told you all."

Elsa had ceased crying. She threw open the window, and leaning out gazed at the garden in all its spring beauty, bathed in the silver moonlight. A nightingale sang sweetly in the linden-tree, and her heart beat almost to bursting. He thought of her! He had spoken of her on the most miserable day of her young life! Oh, what great, all too great happiness!

And then she drew back, closed the window with a bang, and burying her face in her hands burst into tears. Of what use was it? She was only a poor girl!

XVII.

THE little Moravian sat opposite the stately lady, in the simple room. The faces of both were red; they could not agree. Mrs. von Ratenow had thought to find an ally, but on the contrary had encountered, if not an enemy, yet a power which seemed inclined to remain perfectly neutral, and which, although acknowledging the truth of much which the old lady emphasized in her decided way, yet pleaded in favor of Elsa. The calm little person answered her like Moritz himself, although, perhaps, a trifle more soothingly.

"Pray cease, my dear woman," she at last interrupted the sister's gentle speech impatiently; "we do not understand each other. I see that. You may be right from your standpoint, and, besides, you cannot judge my position and the child's. You turn here in a continual circle around your simple interests; we live in the world, and the world has claims even upon Elsa."

"But at the price of peace, which is higher than all prudence!" was the reply.

Mrs. von Ratenow rose.

"I should like to sleep," said she. "I hope that, at

least, you will do nothing *against* my wishes. Elsa must go home with me to-morrow ; she must."

" Certainly, Baroness ; Elsa shall decide herself."

" I think I will be able to conquer the defiant girl," added the old lady ; " but tell me, my dear sister, have you a physician and apothecary in the place ? "

" Certainly ! Do you feel ill, Baroness ? "

" Oh, it will pass ; it is only in case of accident. Sometimes I have an attack which renders me incapable of moving ; and the air in the train was horrible. But we will hope for the best."

" But I will prepare you a little lotion——"

" Oh, not yet, thank you ; only in case of necessity. I have not much faith in such remedies. At home no doctor comes near me. My shepherd is much more reliable ; he can rub and command and conjure away ailments. Why do you stare at me so ? It is true, my dear woman. I will not see Elsa ; I have had enough excitement to-day. Tell her to come to my room to-morrow ; the other girl is probably with her? Well, good-night, then."

They had reached the old lady's bedroom, and with the last words she closed the door in the face of the little Moravian. Sister Beata heard her groan once, as though she were in pain. She shook her head, and went on to the next door.

Miss Lili had seated herself at the table between the windows, was eating bread and butter and soft-boiled eggs and drinking a glass of milk with all the appetite of youth.   Elsa sat near, her eyes red with weeping, and without participating in the meal, watched the moths that were burning their wings over the modest candle. Lili's dainty little figure started up quickly from the chair as Sister Beata entered, and she curtseyed to the grave, simple woman as though she stood before a ruling princess.

"I come to wish you good-night," said Sister Beata ; "to-morrow morning you are to speak to your aunt, Elizabeth ; she hopes that you will accompany her home.   I urge you once more to give prayerful consideration to your resolve.   Good-night, my dear children ; God protect you ! "

Lili stared at her with wide-open eyes, then turned to Elsa, who looked sadder than ever.

"Elsa, is it true ; is there a kind of biscuit here which they call ' brother and sister's hearts,' and, when the dough is extra good, even ' loving brother and sister's hearts ' ? "   And she seated herself and went on eating with great satisfaction.   " Please, please, let me have a couple for breakfast to-morrow morning, and the ' loving ' kind ; I should be so pleased."

A smile crossed Elsa's sad face.   " You are incorrigible, Lili," said she.

"Oh, thank God," cried the mobile little maiden, "you can still laugh !   Oh, Elsa, Elsa," and she knelt down before the girl, "you are all so pious, and have not the least bit of confidence in God !   And yet I know that all will be well with you, I know it very well."

"You know it?" asked Elsa.

"Yes!"

"How do you know?"

"I cannot explain; it is in the air, in the spring air, perhaps, in the flowers and foliage out there, where the birds sing and the water ripples. Ah, well, poor heart, forget your torment; it will all, all come right!"

Elsa shook her head, and gazed at the fresh, girlish face, whose dark eyes shone with tears.

"You are surprised at me, Elsa? Have I always seemed so superficial to you? I tell you quite frankly that I did not trouble myself about you, you were so fearfully tiresome with your grief for your only love, long lost, and so forth—you were so terribly passive. But when I saw you so pale and miserable in spite of your fortunate engagement, which every one lauded to the skies, I was sorry for you; and when you ran away yesterday, you won my whole heart at once, for that was something quite out of the common. Elsa, every one would not do that; a hundred others would have calmly let the net be tightened around them, and would have become Mrs. von Hegebach. But now rely upon me, Elsa, I will help you—and Moritz will help you; even Frieda is no longer quite so angry with you."

"Was she angry with me?" asked Elsa, in astonishment.

"Why, child, were you blind?" cried Lili. "Angry? She was furious, furiously jealous of you whenever

Moritz even mentioned your name. The poor thing
had a hard time of it."

Elsa's pale face had flushed crimson. Suddenly the
young wife's manner, which had seemed so puzzling to
her, was revealed in a glaring light, as was Moritz's shy
avoidance. She groaned in pain, "That also !"

"Calm yourself, sweet child; there was a touching
scene of reconciliation yesterday between the married
couple. Frieda cried like a school-girl, and Moritz
asked again and again, ' Do you see, Frieda, how foolish you were?' And she cried *pater peccavi*, more
gently than I would ever have believed possible in her.
And you will come back with us to-morrow, Elsa, will
you not ? You will not stay here ? It must be horribly
tiresome among all the loving brother and sister's hearts.
You see, this is what I think. The Bennewitzer has
noticed something ; and if he asks, Moritz will tell him
the whole truth, and then the engagement cannot be
continued. Come back, Elsa, dear Elsa."

" No," said the girl, rising, "never ; I cannot."

Lila was about to answer, when a heavy object was
thrown against the door leading into the next room.

"Old people want to sleep," thundered Mrs. von
Ratenow. "Stop talking ; I am worn out !"

Elsa silently went to bed. Lili giggled continuously.
Aunt Ratenow's resolute character was an inexhaustible
source of amusement for her.

In the night she started up ; the moon shone brightly
into the room, and from the other bed she heard soft

sobs. She touched the silky blonde hair, which lay spread over the white pillow. "Elsa, Elsa, are you crying?" she asked softly. Then all was still.

Mrs. von Ratenow was awakened the next morning. A special letter came for her; the little principal herself laid it in her hands.

"Merciful Heaven, the Bennewitzer's hand-writing! How did he learn that she is here?" Her limbs felt like lead; with difficulty she raised herself in bed. "Please, Sister Beata, my spectacles—I cannot move."

The little Moravian handed them to her, and then left her alone. All was quiet in the room; only the soft rustle of the paper in the old lady's hand was heard.

They were only a few words which she read, but the reader's face grew white to the lips. Suddenly she held her hand before her eyes; she grew dizzy. All in vain! All was over!

"Lili!" she cried; her voice sounded like a groan. The young girl came quickly, still in her dressing-gown, with loosened hair. "Give that to Elsa, and hurry and dress yourself." She handed her the letter.

"Do you wish to set out at once, aunt? Shall I tell Elsa?"

"Elsa?" She started up from the pillows. "What have I to do with Elsa? Who sows wind must reap a storm! I hate ingratitude and obstinacy with all my heart."

"Aunt!" cried Lili, terribly frightened at the expression of the old lady's face.

"Go !" cried the old lady ; "we leave in an hour."

The girl stood trembling before Elsa, who was just fastening up her blonde braids. "Elsa!" she said. "Oh, heavens, aunt is so angry, so angry !"

The little hand dropped the heavy braids and seized the paper.

"MY DEAR MADAM :

"In all haste—the letter is to go by this mail. I beg you to give my cousin back her liberty in my name. The rest by word of mouth—later. Yours sincerely,

"H. VON HEGEBACH."

For a moment the girl's chest heaved as though freed from a fearful weight. Then she buried her face in her hands, and a shudder shook her frame.

"Elsa, Elsa!" cried Lili, clasping her in her arms. But Elsa freed herself and turned the knob of the door leading to Mrs. von Ratenow's room. The door was locked.

"Is it you, Lili ?" asked the old lady.

"No, it is Elsa, aunt," she cried pleadingly.

All was silence.

"Aunt," sobbed the girl, her voice half-suffocated.

Again no answer. Only steps were heard, and hasty preparations for departure.

"Aunt, a word !" Her hand pulled and turned at the knob as though in deathly terror. In vain. She gave up her efforts ; for a moment she remained motionless, her eyes fixed upon the window, then looked at

Lili. It seemed as though she wished to smile but tears rushed to her eyes, and a full consciousness of her desolateness overcame her at this moment. Now in truth she had nothing left her in the world.

An hour later, Mrs. von Ratenow paced up and down the platform of the railway station, leaning on Lili's arm, as they waited for the train. The old lady was suffering; one could see that, by the lips so tightly pressed together. She felt far from happy; she could have wept if she had known how. She had wept once in her life, not when her husband was laid in his grave, but when she had taken a little crying child from her dead mother, in her own arms. " There is no gratitude in the world." And she began to find fault with the train for being so late, with the porters for staring at her, with the despicable coffee at the school, and her aching head; while Lili walked silently beside her, with a miserable face and tearful eyes, and turned as often as possible to look back at the pointed gables of the house half-hidden among the trees, as though she must see a window open and a girl's head leaning out gazing over the landscape with longing eyes.

> " And nothing else have I to claim or to keep
> Save only two brown eyes with which I may weep."

Lili could not banish from her thoughts to-day these words which Elsa had once sung. And then came the train.

Eight days later a gentleman passed the little lonely

Moravian village, in the express train. The train did
not stop, but the young man stood at the window of the
coupé, and gazed out as intently as though it were the
most beautiful country through which he was being
whirled. Then he seated himself, pushed aside a violin-
case, drew out his pocket-book and taking from it a
letter began to read :

"MY DEAR BERNARDI :

"You have placed a pistol at my breast, and although I do
not like to write letters, least of all letters of a sentimental nature,
I will nevertheless attempt it if it will satisfy you as you say.

" There is little satisfactory about the matter—for you, that is. I
confess that my hardened soldier heart was somewhat touched as
I thought of a certain ball evening when I felt called upon to give
you some good advice.

" It is really true : little Elsa von Hegebach, one morning very
early, left her warm nest in the castle, the most devoted of aunts,
and a paternal *fiancé*, in order to weep in the quiet of a Moravian
colony, over—I do not know what, perhaps you may. All sensible
people, and you know how many such persons our city walls are
fortunate enough to contain, shrug their shoulders and smile.   It
is no longer the fashion nowadays to take to one's heels from a
wealthy lover ; romances now begin at the other side of the altar,
and then it is so much more piquant.   The resolute little girl has
drawn down upon herself the greatest displeasure of old Mrs. von
Ratenow, who with her practical views of life, cherishes justified
doubts as to her adopted child's sanity.   She herself has returned
seriously ill from her pursuit.   She was carried from the carriage
to her bed.   According to all reports to-day she is still far from
well.

" I need not assure you that our society, especially the little clique
of ladies, have ample material for gossip ; and that the name

' Bernardi ' is frequently mentioned, you perhaps suspect. And alas, with right ! ''Tis that which saddens my heart !' says a poet. For what is to come of it all ? It is a pity about the pretty girl, but who is to blame ? It is not your, and not her fault. It is all on account of money, everything depends upon money. Why are you not a wealthy baron, with a half-dozen estates ? Why does man need so much for his pitiful existence ? Yes, why ? I will cease to question ; I am really becoming sentimental. I cannot banish from my thoughts the little girl with the longing brown eyes. You should have seen her the day of the funeral.

" Do not think that I regret having told you the truth at that time; assuredly not, it was my duty. She will probably forget, even although less easily than others. And do not despair ; you cannot help her. Man is the slave of his circumstances.

." Farewell, Bernardi.

" Yours,

" VON ROST."

How often the letter had already been read ; how often ? Now it was put back in his pocket, and the owner sat and stared at one spot as though he could there find the answer to the " why ? " contained in the letter. A number of plans passed through the young man's mind ; he gnashed his teeth in mad rage. "The slave of his circumstances " !

The train rushed past a station at the edge of a forest. In the warm May sun, under the young leaved birches, sat on the door-sill a young woman with a child in her lap. The man stood at the gates, and the young woman gazed smilingly at the train as it rushed on. Suddenly, bitter envy overcame him. The children of the people love each other, marry, and are happy ; if they have

nothing to eat, they are hungry together as they work
together. And why not? Elsa too would have worked
with him, and hungered with him; he had read that in
her dear eyes. Absurd! The children of rank dragged
behind them the heavy velvet robe of duties of their
rank, which, made up of thousands of bits and frag-
ments, forms a magnificent whole. This robe seems so
incomparably comfortable and agreeable to the wealthy,
but so weighs upon the poor that only with great difficulty is it kept upon the shoulders; but yet one dare not
be seen in these higher circles without it—oh, no!
How much misery and grief, how many disappointed
hopes, how much renunciation it covers!

It is so necessary! Without this robe, society cannot
be thought of; it belongs to it; it would be absurd to con-
tradict this. The majority wear it so easily; the few
who fancy they are suffocating under it—pah! Well,
they suffocate, but they finally become accustomed to
it. Elsa will console herself; and for him—perhaps
there will soon be a war.

"Elsa will not console herself!" said an inner voice,
"Elsa will mourn away her youth, and become a solitary, embittered old maid, the sunny, charming girl."
And he pondered on almost feverishly, as for so many
previous days. But what could he do? Should he
choose another profession?

Then suddenly Mrs. von Ratenow stood before him,
and her diamonds sparkled as on that evening.

"Do you believe that in another calling one can live

on air? And do you believe that you will be satisfied when you have put off the gay coat?"

And now, as countless times before, he fancied himself a merchant—without capital? A farmer—to remain an inspector for his whole life? Artist—should he increase the throng of those who never rise above mediocrity, and are bitter and depressed because they feel that they will never reach their desired aim? It sounded pitiless but yet was true.

Rather would he resign, and seek his fortune across the ocean. But his old father, and his mother who had saved every penny to fulfil his ardent desire to be a soldier!

Farewell, ye dreams; farewell, Elsa! The slave of his circumstances—what can a slave do?

"He has come back more irritable than he went away," said his comrades, when the next morning, after review, they walked down the street to their barracks. "Foolish fellow! He really still clings to his unhappy love," added one, smiling; "incredible at the present day!"

XVIII.

It was again autumn. The wind carried on a mad frolic with the leaves in the castle garden, and the clusters of wild grapes over the veranda were deep purple. A small fire burned on the hearth in old Mrs. von Ratenow's room, and the inmate sat, erect as ever, at the window knitting and gazing into the yard. Her face was no longer so full ; she had changed, her severe illness in the spring had not been without effect upon her. Slowly, slowly she had recovered. She had been in Baden-Baden the past summer, only to be terribly homesick there. Frieda and Lili who accompanied her—Moritz had remained at home—had had full opportunity to change their gowns three times a day, to take promenades and excursions with their rapidly made acquaintances. She was happy to sit alone in the garden before the house, and hear nothing of the silly noise and commotion.

At home, things went better. Aunt Lott was there again, and could express herself very plainly when the topic of conversation was Elsa. And Aunt Lott never wearied of referring to this topic again and again.

"You must admit that I am in the right, Lott. The child, in her sinful petulance, has trampled her happiness under foot."

"Yes, my dear Ratenow—but——"

"'But'? There is no 'but' to the matter, I should think. Well, let her eat what she has cooked. To compromise herself and all of us in such a manner!"

"Dear Ratenow, how can you speak so?" concluded Aunt Lott, tearfully. "How can you refuse to read her letters? She writes so that tears come to my eyes when I merely look at them."

And no answer followed, but the conversation ended only to be begun and ended in the same manner a few days later.

Aunt Lott corresponded very industriously with the poor darling. She reported every trifle of castle news, and conscientiously delivered all messages with which Elsa commissioned her. But one of the child's wishes she could not fulfil; the old lady could not obtain a friendly word from Aunt Ratenow, and she could give Elsa no certainty as to whether the Bennewitzer was too terribly angry with her.

The Bennewitzer was completely inexplicable. He came to see Mrs. von Ratenow as before, and recently they had played cribbage together. He calmly smoked his cigar in the drawing-room, and once surprised the old lady with the information that he now, like a true grandfather, had provided himself at home with a dressing-gown and long pipe.

15

"But my dear Hegebach!" Mrs. von Ratenow stared at him incredulously, in her eyes he was still so young and handsome; but nevertheless it seemed to her that the hair on his temples was very gray. He had never asked after Elsa. But when Aunt Lott, who at the girl's request, often visited her parents' graves, reached the mounds, they were always covered with the loveliest flowers; and the sexton's wife told that the Bennewitzer gentleman had done this. Aunt Lott had learned this with a certain satisfaction, and had thanked him for it. "Why thank me?" he asked; "they are my relatives."

For the rest, everything went on as usual in the castle. Frieda now had a governess for her children, danced and went into society as in the past year. Moritz played his whist and chatted with his mother— only the apple of discord was out of the house. The light, girlish tread was no longer heard on the stairs. Elsa could come down stairs so prettily; it was really no walk, it was rather a flying, the lovely figure was suddenly down-stairs no one knew how. She no longer sang her little songs in the drawing-room, or played hide-and-seek with the children in the deep window recesses. Something was missing; something lovely, charming. That, all felt, but no one spoke of it. Only sometimes, in the twilight, Aunt Lott fancied that the door must open, and she rush in and call in her clear, ringing voice, "Aunt Lott, dear Auntie Lott!" And sometimes Mrs. von Ratenow started up as

though she heard that voice, but anxiously and pleadingly, "Aunt, only a word, a word!" and then she felt so strangely, half-angry, half-mournful.

No! If anything were now to be made of the girl she must be stern with her. The Bennewitzer was assuredly of her opinion; and perhaps she would yet become submissive in that melancholy nest.

To-day the house was quiet; Frieda and Lili had come to show themselves to the old lady in their elegant silk gowns, with their flowers and laces in all the splendor of gala toilets; both dressed alike in pale-blue and silver down to their dainty slippers. They held huge bouquets in their hands, and the yellow *gloire de Dijon* roses adorned their dark hair and corsages.

Annie Cramm was to be married to-day.

The wedding was to take place at three o'clock, the dinner at four, and the whole city was on the *qui vive* to see the bridal party enter the church. There were such fabulous rumors of the splendor which was to be seen; and Aunt Lott had sat in the church since half-past one so as to secure a good place.

Old Mrs. von Ratenow was quite alone; she thought of the pair who were probably at that moment being married, and what an unenviable wife Annie Cramm would make, however much brocade and lace she might wear. What a commonplace arrangement it was; a marriage without the slightest mutual interests. Well, they had wished nothing better, and could pass life very comfortably ; at least they would have no cares. And her thoughts flew to Elsa ; she saw the girl beside Bernardi, and heard her laugh. Involuntarily her imagination replaced the other couple, who were now probably occupying the seats of honor at the abundantly-spread table in the bride's home, with these two. And suddenly this table stood yonder in the hall, and she sat opposite them, and——

"Such nonsense !" She coughed quite loudly and began to knit. But the picture was so attractive ; it came back to her mental view. Could there be anything more beautiful than such a young, newly-married couple, who loved each other with all their hearts ?

"Yes, yes ; Elsa was really no worse than Annie Cramm, only she had no money. Nonsense ! One must adapt oneself to circumstances ! "

Gradually twilight came on. A carriage rolled into the yard.

" The Bennewitzer ? Oh, I thought he would be at the dinner ! " But he came in and kissed her hand. "What then ?" she asked. "Is it over already ? "

"Oh, not at all, my dear madam ! " And he drew his chair quite near the old lady's window seat. " I only desired to talk with you, to lay bare my heart to you."

She pricked up her ears—at last he spoke. She could excuse Elsa, she could—good heavens—perhaps—she dared not finish even in thought.

" The dinner truly was excellent and the wines

exquisite. One must acknowledge that old **Mr. Cramm** has taste. The bridegroom certainly behaved strangely for one so lately married ; at dessert he suddenly left his fairer half and seated himself beside me."

"Strange, assuredly ! " agreed the old lady.

"Yes; was it not? He does not talk badly, has sensible views and seems practical."

"He has proved that to-day," remarked Mrs. von Ratenow, dryly.

"Eh ? Oh, yes—well—*chacun à son goût.* He spoke of Elsa to-day."

At length her name had crossed his lips.

"She sent a little present yesterday. But it was not of that that I wished to speak with you, dear Mrs. von Ratenow ; pardon the digression."

Mrs. von Ratenow looked at him in surprise. Had the Bennewitzer taken too much of the " exquisite " wine ?

" I do not know whether you can put yourself in my place," he continued, smoking comfortably. " I hardly believe so—or yes ? Women have an advantage ; they are more sympathetic than the so-called stronger sex. I feel so indescribably lonely. I do not know for whom I live and work. My whole house has a melancholy look to me, as though every chimney-place opens its mouth in a monstrous yawn, and asks me : for what purpose am I here ? It cannot go on longer thus, my dear Mrs. von Ratenow, for it makes me mentally and physically ill." He was silent for a moment. "But I

have Bennewitz on my shoulders, and so I have thought
of once more —— "

He was silent.   The ashes had fallen from his cigar
upon his clothes ; calmly he brushed them off.

" Marrying ? "—the old lady completed his sentence
anxiously.

" No ! " said he shortly, leaning back in his chair.

Mrs. von Ratenow turned and looked at him.   It was
now quite dark ; she could only see that he was looking
past her and out of the window.

" No ? "

" Certainly not ; I think of doing something quite
different, something which does not concern me so
nearly, and in which I need fear no harsh rejection—for
that is painful.   You know no one is without vanity,
and in spite of all prudent reasoning, a sting remains."

The old lady sat in breathless expectation.

" I wish once more to try to bind a young life to
mine, but in another manner—I wish to adopt a child."

It flashed upon the old lady like lightning.

" Hegebach, you would—you could—? " cried she
joyously.   Then she paused.   " But girls were pro-
hibited from inheriting ? " said she doubtfully.

" Girls ?   Who spoke of a girl ? " he asked.

No answer ; only a quick, deep breath.   The man was
right ; why had Elsa behaved so unwarrantably.   But it
is bitter, bitter !   Oh, the unhappy child !

" What do you say to my plan, my dear Mrs. von
Ratenow ? "

"Excellent!" she replied with difficulty; and grief for the poor girl, who now must really make her way through life alone, extinguished almost all anger in her heart.

"But now I must search for a suitable person," said the Bennewitzer.

"You will find many applicants."

"Oh, assuredly!" He laughed shortly. "A little bit of wealth makes them spring up like mushrooms after a rain. It would be really delightful to find people who would say 'No!' Eh? But in any case I will submit my choice to you for approval, and I shall begin my search at once. Apropos, how is my cousin?"

"I—I do not know; I suppose she is well," answered Mrs. von Ratenow. The Bennewitzer's manner fairly enraged her to-day.

"Good heavens, my dear madam, you are not angry with her still? It is wrong in you, really! Do you know that I have in thought asked the child's pardon a thousand times for our sins against her? Yes, I say our, my dear Mrs. von Ratenow; you, my cousin, and I sinned against her. Our only excuse is that we meant well."

"Of what use is that to her?" thought the old woman.

"I must take leave of you now." He rose. "You think I am doing right, do you not? One must have some one to love and care for."

"Yes, yes, my dear Hegebach; and may you never regret it."

And when the door had closed behind him, the old
lady remained standing in the middle of the room.
"Either he has taken too much wine, or he has become
a trifle crazy in his old age ; they are all slightly crazy,
the Hegebachs." That same evening she wrote a letter
to Elsa. The poor child ! To be deprived of everything ! But it was her own fault. It was a strange
letter, half reproachful, half tender, and containing the
request that the girl would soon return.

The old lady did not close her eyes that night. The
next day she went about with a very thoughtful air ; at
dinner she scarcely spoke a word, and yet the principal
topic of conversation was the Bennewitzer's newest
project.

"The man is perfectly right," said Moritz. "Of
course he wishes to leave his property to a man of
whom he is fond, and who is legally entitled to it; otherwise it will revert to the government. But he could
leave Elsa something from his private property," he
added.

"Yes," assented Aunt Lott. "It is an ignoble re-
venge to thus leave her to her fate, for he is her
cousin."

"As though Elsa would accept it ! " Lili drew down
her little mouth scornfully.

"Oho ! " said Mrs. von Ratenow, who until then had
been silent. "She will know now very well what it means
to look out for herself ; she will gladly accept it, but he
would be a fool to give it, I think."

"You do not believe that yourself, mother," said Moritz, taking her hand.

Mrs. van Ratenow had ordered her carriage immediately after dinner. To her son's great amazement it stopped before the steps.

"Where are you going, mother dear?" he asked as the old lady came out in her fur cloak and hood—the autumn day was cool—followed by a servant with wraps and lap-robe.

"To drive," she replied shortly.

Moritz did not answer; he knew her manner too well; she had something particular in view. He respectfully helped her into the carriage, but was forced to suppress a smile. It was such disagreeable weather which had enticed his mother out to drive.

The carriage rolled out of the yard; Mrs. von Ratenow was still busy in wrapping herself up warmly. At the city gate she threw off the wraps and looked out of the window. "Drive to Büstrow John—but a little more quickly."

The carriage rolled along in the dictated direction ; the young fruit-trees at both sides of the road skimmed past the solitary woman's gaze ; the autumn wind rattled the carriage windows ; far in the distance the Büstrow church-tower rose above the tree-tops. It all looked so dreary, the autumnal landscape under the cloudy sky ; and John drove on. Close to Büstrow his mistress ordered him to stop.

" Is that the road to Bennewitz ? " she asked.

" Yes, madam ! "

" Drive there, John."

John turned and drove quickly, for the first drops of rain fell, and from the black clouds one could see that the storm would be severe. In ten minutes, John drew up before the stately old gabled house. A servant sprang out and helped Mrs. von Ratenow to alight.

" It is I, Seeben," she nodded to the surprised old man. " Is the master at home ? "

" Yes. Will the Baroness come in ? "

" You may drive to the stable, John," she ordered the coachman, and entered the house. She was well acquainted with it from former times, but, nevertheless, she was surprised at its air of comfort and elegance. What a beautiful house in the course of years the Bennewitzer had made of the neglected old rattle-trap ! And what a splendid estate the so-called sandbank had become under his management !

" Foolish Elsa ! " she murmured, as she stood in the drawing-room, so elegant, cosey, and comfortable, as

only a man can make his surroundings when he has taste, a sense of the beautiful, and abundant means at his disposal.

"I will tell the Baron at once," whispered the servant, and drew one of the soft easy-chairs to the fire. "He is engaged for the moment."

Mrs. von Ratenow seated herself and gazed at the large picture over the chimney. "His first wife," she said to herself. "Hegebach always had good taste," she thought, looking at the woman's figure, which seemed stepping out of the frame towards her. A queenly-looking figure in a soft white gown, her head slightly thrown back, so that her face was shown in profile ; in the background the Bennewitz house was visible through the trees. On the mantel-piece, at the foot of the picture, was a *jardinière* filled with rare and fragrant roses.

"He surely loved her very dearly," thought the old lady ; "and would it not be hard for her successor to be forced to share her husband's attentions with the dead. Ah, he will never marry again ! "

She was roused from her thoughts, for loud conversation was heard in the adjoining room. Immediately after the door opened, and a lady of about forty years entered, followed by a slender, handsome boy of perhaps fifteen. They passed Mrs. von Ratenow, with a silent bow. She looked after them with varied feelings, half astonished, half disappointed. Suddenly she shook her head and murmured, "Ah, indeed ! " as though

she had discovered something important, although
hardly agreeable. She felt decidedly uncomfortable
and believed that her coming here had been useless,
that she herself and all that she wished were terribly
superfluous.

Then the Bennewitzer stood before her, and drew
her hand to his lips.

"My dear Mrs. von Ratenow, to what do I owe the
unusual honor of a visit from you?"

"Yes, I do not wonder that you ask, Hegebach. It
is strange in me so suddenly to fall upon you; is it
not?"

"It is charming, my dear madam!"

He pressed her down in her chair again, and seated
himself opposite her.

"I cannot stay long, Hegebach. I am afraid that I
disturbed you—in an important moment."

"Not at all; the matter was already arranged," he
replied.

"He is a handsome boy, Hegebach."

"The one who just passed through here?" he asked.
"Oh, a splendid fellow!"

"He is, indeed!" she assented. Then they were
silent; the Bennewitzer had gone to ring the bell.

Now he returned. "I am very glad that you have
come, Mrs. von Ratenow," he began; "otherwise I
should probably have gone to you. I am uneasy and
excited; you know why. It is a step which is not to
be considered unimportant. Suddenly to wish to place

a stranger at your side ; to expect of him all that which
only the ties of relationship are justified in demanding,
love, consideration, reverence ; to be to this stranger all
that one had been to one's own children—it is something peculiar, my dear madam, and it is not easy ; do
you think so ? "

The old lady nodded. Her thoughts still dwelt upon
the boy who had passed through the room shortly before. She could no longer be in doubt. " Pardon me,
Hegebach," she began, drawing a deep breath ; "was
the handsome little fellow one of the candidates for the
position of your son ? "

" Who ? "

" The one who with his mother——"

" Oh no, no, my dear Mrs. von Ratenow ! I am his
guardian and am greatly interested in him ; he was my
poor Henry's best friend, but——"

" Forgive me, Hegebach ! "

Mrs. von Ratenow drew a fresh breath.

" But I have entered into negotiations elsewhere
already, and await news hourly."

The old lady again writhed with uneasiness. "Well,
my dear Hegebach, I wish you all happiness ! " Suddenly she rose ; it was already quite dark. "I must
hurry home ; they do not know where I am ; there is no
need for me to remain longer—you will pardon me,
Hegebach. I came to make you a proposition—I—had
a plan. Now it is too late. I meant no harm, Hegebach."

He did not answer. All was silence in the room; only the heavy silk rustled as she fastened her mantle, and the clock ticked softly.

"Good-by, Hegebach. You know old women love to pry into other persons' affairs, but it was well meant."

He followed her silently to the door. "Why in such haste?" he at length asked, constrainedly. "Will you not take some refreshment, my dear Mrs. von Rate-now?"

She declined. She had already seized the door knob; then she drew back a step. The old servant entered with a lamp, and handed the Baron a despatch.

"A moment, my dear madam," he urged, and going up to the lamp, tore open the envelope. "Read it!" said he then. "I am again unfortunate," and he handed her the paper.

She raised her eye-glass, and read:

"Declines; persuasions useless.
"VON ROST."

"What does that mean?" she asked hastily.

"A refusal from the son of my choice." He had paled.

Aunt Ratenow stared at the despatch; her eyes shone. She read the name of the place from which it was sent, she read the signature, and her old heart beat joyously.

"And you are very anxious for this one?"

"For this one, just for this one," said he; "very anxious!"

"Give me power, Hegebach. You scarcely know him; let me——"

"I really do not know him at all," said he; "one fact alone determined me to choose him, that——"

"Hegebach!" The old lady went up to the man still standing beside the table, his hand resting upon it as if in deep thought. "Hegebach!" She wished to continue, but suddenly began to weep. She wept for joy, and was immediately angry with herself for shedding such copious tears. Nothing was more vexatious to her than to be discovered in an act of soft-heartedness, and she dried her eyes resolutely and began to scold. "I really should leave you to your own devices, Hegebach; really! What a sly fellow you are! But it is always thus, my dear man, when two of the so-called stronger sex put their heads together to accomplish something very clever. Rost! He must have talked well; you could not find a better ambassador! Why did I learn nothing of this? Confess, Hegebach!"

He smiled. "We wished to surprise you, dear Mrs. von Ratenow, for you surely had not thought of him."

"Indeed?" said she, laughing amid her tears. "But nevertheless, old Mrs. Ratenow is the best one to attend to the matter now."

Yes, that she was. Late in the evening Moritz learned that his mother wished to set out on a journey the next morning. She did set out, and returned after three days. Then the Bennewitzer came, and they left together. This time the others at least learned their destination ; they went to Berlin.

"Mamma wishes to procure a son for the Bennewitzer as she was unsucessful in obtaining a wife for him," declared Frieda. "If I could only explain one fact satisfactorily, Moritz——"

"And that is ?"

"I always thought that mamma was anxious to marry him off merely for Elsa's sake. But why she assists him in adopting a son is a mystery to me. It does not concern her, eh, Moritz ?"

Moritz was ungallant enough not to answer. He merely whistled softly to himself.

In the evening Von Rost and his bride came to the house. Outside it rained and stormed, but Frieda's blue boudoir was delightfully cosey.

They had soon returned from their wedding trip. Annie had already travelled extensively, and the weather was bad ; besides Rost had made out such a remarkable route. Instead of going to Vienna, he had taken his young wife to the obscure town of H——, and then he had vanished for a half-day completely. "To buy a horse," he had told Annie afterwards; for with the cavalry, horse-dealings were undoubtedly justifiable even on a honey-moon. Annie related this, half laughing, half vexed. But the monster had capped the climax by taking her to Berlin, "to Berlin, which I know as well as my native city. Then I lost patience. Do you know, we saw your mother-in-law there ?" she concluded.

"Yes, mamma has a secret mission there." And Frieda shook her head.

"The Bennewitzer was also in Berlin," said Annie.

"Bernardi also sent his regards to every one," interposed the young husband, adjusting his eye-glass to look at Frieda.

"In Berlin?" cried she, with unfeigned astonishment. And Moritz laughed in his sleeve. Then he excused himself; he wished to meet his mother at the railway station.

"So, my boy," said she, as an hour later she sat beside her son in the carriage, which rolled quickly along through the dark winter evening to the castle. "Now all is arranged. But it took great trouble in all directions. Will you believe it, Moritz; Hegebach even had to apply to the Emperor. What absurd laws men have made to render life more hard! In a few weeks the Bennewitzer will have a son, Moritz; and what a son!"

ELSA VON HEGEBACH was just leaving the school-room.

It was winter. The little Moravian village lay solitary. Through the bare branches of the trees one could plainly see the distant mountains which already had snow on their summits. In the school-room wood fires crackled and the lamps must be lighted early.

Around and ahead of Elsa rushed perhaps thirty little girls, sprang about in the freshly-fallen snow in the garden, with true delight, and immediately began a heated combat with snow-balls. The young girl remained standing in the house door, watching the flying balls and the romping children. A smile crossed her pale face ; she had also once frolicked thus. She drew in a deep breath of bracing cold air ; it did her good after the close school-room.

Then she crossed the garden to the rear of the house, and mounted the creaking stairs ; now she was alone in her room, and the best hour of the day had arrived for her. Then she read or wrote letters, or sat at the window, gazing out into the distance, and thought. Yes, of what does one think when one is alone, and nearby a violin sings old sweet melodies? And Miss Brown, the English teacher, was accustomed to play all sorts of music on her violin. Sometimes Elsa could not bear to hear it ; those were the days when heartache and longing overcame her with full force, the days when she thought she could not bear life. Then her poor head and heart ached, and her eyes pained from hopeless weeping. And she asked herself why she alone was miserable, so miserable?

Then she fled from the tones of the violin, and ran out into the storm and rain, how far she did not know. Or she went to Sister Beata's room, and sat there silently for hours.

" I cannot listen to the violin, Sister Beata."

" But I will give you another room, Elizabeth."

" No, no ! " she replied hastily.

To-day, as if sunk in thought, she stood before the simple bureau, whose upper drawer she had pulled out. She took up several papers and seated herself with them at the window. She read them again, these letters which she had received perhaps eight weeks ago, and which had given her such food for thought.

"Dear Elsa :

"You know that I was not angry with you for my sake, but because you acted against your own interests, and not well. However that cannot be changed ; you must bear what you have brought upon yourself, and God will surely provide for you, although I am not pious enough to believe that our whole path of life is already mapped out by Him like an architect's plan, even while we are infants.

"That is a belief for Turks !

"I say God gave us intelligence that we might act and judge. You have not used your intelligence rightly, but allowed your foolish heart to conquer you. The consequences are worse than I expected, but a truce to this ! You will learn them soon enough, and will not be spared remorse——

"Now I beg you, Elsa, to come back again ! You shall not lose your home. Free yourself from your engagement there. You are needed here, and the bread offered you is not the proverbial bread of strangers which has seven crusts.

"I think you will come soon ; the winter evenings are long, and I should like to have you read to me as you did last year. God bless you ! Always your loving,

"Aunt Ratenow."

She shook her head. "No !" said she aloud, and laid aside the letter. "I am no trained poodle which jumps over a cane held out to him. No !"

She sat still for a while, then took up the second letter; it was in Lili's scrawling handwriting. She glanced over the description of Annie Cramm's wedding, and her eyes rested on the conclusion of the letter:

"A telegram from Bernardi also arrived," she read. "But now wonder, Elsa ; the newly-made husband seems to have conceived a remarkable liking for the Bennewitzer ! He suddenly

left his dear wife, and seated himself beside him, directly opposite me. They chatted away briskly but most impolitely, in an undertone. During the time, I could not take my eyes from the Bennewitzer. Finally they shook hands and separated. The Bennewitzer disappeared after the supper, and, as I learned later, went to see Aunt Ratenow. But now, Elsa, comes what I really wanted to tell you. I have no more hope, for the Bennewitzer intends 'retiring.' Do you know what that means in such a case? He has already bargained for a grandfather's chair; he will never marry again. He is about *to adopt a son!* Your aunt says this is very sensible, but at heart she is raging, that I can see, for she had intended, my love, that you should reside at Bennewitz.

"And her leaving you in D——refusing to forgive you—that was only a last effort; she wished to tame you by hunger. This is the state of affairs.

"Ah, dearest Elsa, I fear we will both die old maids, and I have no talent for it like Aunt Lott; she is a born old maid—— "

Yes, that she was! Aunt Ratenow had wished to tame her, now the Bennewitzer had drawn a stroke through the reckoning himself, thank God! No, no, aunt had always meant kindly toward her, but go back to her—never! She thought of all the wakeful nights, the wretched hours which she had passed there, and then the recollections—" No!" She unfolded a third letter, which she had written herself; it was the draft of her answer to Aunt Ratenow:

"MY DEAR AUNT:

"Accept many thanks for your kind words which have pleased and relieved me unspeakably. It was very hard for me to have incurred your displeasure, and only the consciousness that I did right, upheld me in all the sad days which followed your departure from here. Accept my warmest thanks for the love which you have always shown me, and which again to-day has been proved to me. How could I ever forget what you have done for me! But do not think me defiant and ungrateful. I remain here —I feel that work is the only thing which can console me for the painful experiences which I have had during the last year—— "

She dropped the sheet. Had she not written too bitterly? she asked herself. But who picks sweet fruit from a sickly, broken tree? Her pen had involuntarily traced these words.

She folded the letter again, and sat there quietly. In the next room the violin was being played upon. Miss Brown seemed very melancholy to-day; she had begun with "Home, sweet home."

She was a lanky, sandy-haired, freckled woman, and her eyes wore a perpetual look of homesickness. Her favorite hours were those of twilight, when she could play her violin, she had told Elsa; and Elsa closed her eyes and to these sounds dreamed of another hand which handled the bow in such a masterly fashion, of tones which were indescribably sweeter and softer.

How vivid it all was! There was the Hungarian dance, and now—how did the English woman come by the German folk-song?

> " Ah, who in this world is like me left to pine.
> No father, no mother, no fortune is mine;
> And nothing else have I——"

She began to weep again. Where did they all come from, these tears?

Now some one mounted the stairs outside; who could it be coming stumbling up in that fashion? Probably the lamp was not yet lighted in the hall. Some one passed her door, heavily; it sounded like a man's tread. There was a knock at the door of the next room; the violin-playing ceased. "Come in!" she heard Miss Brown call, and immediately after, "Dear me!" and a man's deep voice asking apologetically for information.

"The next door if you please, sir," said Miss Brown, in her broken German.

Suddenly Elsa stood in the open doorway, and tried to pierce the deep twilight with her gaze, her hands pressed tightly against her beating heart. "Moritz?" she asked softly and doubtfully.

"Elsa, my dear Elsa, where are you hiding? In this Egyptian darkness one cannot see one's hand before one's face. Yes, my dear girl. You did not expect me."

Yes, that was Moritz's well-known voice. They stood in the little room. Elsa could not yet understand it.

"Moritz, you?" Her trembling fingers lighted the lamp, and now she gazed into his face.

"Yes, I!" And he took off his overcoat upon which the snow-flakes began to melt, and held out both hands to her. "What does he want now? You ask yourself this, eh? He has come to fetch you, you runaway. Without you I dare not present myself at the castle again."

She shook her head, and gazed at him with eyes which told of many tears. He smiled and seated himself comfortably upon a chair near the stove.

"Only for a few days' visit, Elsa. Mother must speak with you. She cannot travel, or else she would have come herself. She is not yet quite herself ; she was very ill in the spring. Therefore she sent me now."

"Aunt wrote to me some time ago," said Elsa.

"And you answered her. I know it."

Elsa flushed. "I could not do otherwise, Moritz!"

"Mother asks nothing more of you, Elsa, than to come with me. You are perfectly free to return here again at any moment."

"I do not know, Moritz, whether I can——"

"You can, Elsa! Only dress yourself warmly and come."

"What are you thinking of, Moritz? So, without all preparation!"

"Oh, I have been conferring with Sister Beata for an hour down-stairs; all is arranged."

"I do not want to go," said she, defiantly.

"Of course not," he replied; "or why are you a Hegebach? Defiance is inbred in that family."

"Moritz!" Her tears came again. "I have been nothing but a trouble and vexation to every one since I came into the world—against my inclination, but so it is; to my father, your mother, and you; yes, Moritz, you too; and you were always so kind. Leave me here; ah, leave me here!"

Suddenly he laughed so heartily and loudly that the violin hushed, as if alarmed, in the next room, in the midst of a brilliant cadenza. "You dear, foolish girl," said he, and took her in his arms. "So you know that, too? Well, to calm you, Frieda first proposed that I should and must fetch you. Aunt Lott offered, but Frieda insisted. Are you satisfied now? Well, cry;

you have fifteen minutes' time for it. And meanwhile, for the sake of science, I will test your famous liquor in the tavern. In a quarter of an hour I shall return, Elsa. And pray give me a light; that old ladder positively endangers one's life in the darkness. Good-by. ·Be ready!"

She seated herself defiantly; she would not. Who could compel her? What right had they to drag her away from her difficultly won peace? And so there she sat when Moritz returned.

His honest blue eyes looked pained and surprised. Then he took out his watch and placed himself beside the stove.

"Ten minutes more," said his lips, but his eyes said, "I had not expected this!"

She rose, took from the wardrobe her jacket and a few articles of clothing, which she placed in a sachel. Then she stood still and gazed around the room; again "I cannot!" rose to her lips. And then suddenly she found herself down-stairs ready for her journey, and gave Sister Beata her hand.

"God keep you, Elizabeth!"

"I shall come back soon, Sister Beata."

"If God pleases!" said the gentle little woman.

It was snowing, and the frosty air fanned the girl's forehead.

"Have you wrapped yourself up warmly, dear?" asked Moritz, anxiously. She nodded, and walked beside him in silence.

They were just in time. Elsa did not know how she got into the bright, warm railway carriage so quickly.

"It is a fast train," said Moritz, as they started. "We have only five hours; at eleven we will be at home."

At home! The girl turned away and gazed out of the window. She had a depressing feeling of false submission, of weakness of character; it made her wretched. He noticed plainly that she did not feel happy, and wished to entertain her.

"I know scarcely any news to tell you, Elsa," he began. "The Rosts entertain a great deal. Madame Annie distinguishes herself by her style and costumes, and Lili is on the verge of betrothal, as she writes my wife. It is an old love, I believe. Her father-in-law has until now bitterly opposed the match. It is a school boy and girl affair—but you probably know this—now fortunately he has obtained a good position in Heidelberg, and she has carried her point, the little witch who always seemed so flighty."

Elsa looked up but said nothing, she felt even more sad.

"Yes, and the Bennewitzer has carried his point. Will you permit me to smoke, Elsa? Thanks. And he possesses an adopted son. Are you too warm, Elsa?"

"Yes; please open the window."

"Mother was forced to put in her word," he continued, and blew his cigar smoke comfortably into the air; "he probably would never have succeeded had she not assisted him. Now he seems quite satisfied."

"I am glad," said she, speaking almost for the first time.

"He is about to have a grand celebration of this event. You can imagine that he is again the talk of the town, Elsa."

Yes, of course! And she too, probably—and she had been foolish enough to come back with Moritz! She wrapped herself closer in her shawl, drew her veil over her face and leaned her head back among the cushions. She was very angry with herself.

And the train rushed on, and Moritz slept. The nearer she came to her destination the more anxious she became, inexplicably anxious. It seemed like a dream to her when she seated herself in the carriage; like an old, sad, and yet so sweet dream. The coachman's "Good evening" had sounded so pleasant to her, and the little coupé smelled so deliciously of Frieda's favorite perfume. Happy old recollections overcame her; her heart beat joyously. She could not help it.

She stood in the lofty hall, half dazed; and Moritz made excuses for Frieda because she was not waiting to receive them. She was probably asleep, and his mother also, but Aunt Lott was waiting upstairs, and in Aunt Lott's doorway stood a dear little figure with outstretched arms.

"Ah, thank God, Elsa, my own darling, that you are here!" was the welcome she received; and the weeping, little aunt clasped her in her arms. "Oh, how lovely that you have come; now all is well!"

How she could talk, dear Aunt Lott; and she forced her to drink some warm tea, while the girl sat there silently, and only at length said, "Do I not smell violets?"

"That is only a fancy, Elsa; that is the perfume of recollection—yes, yes; oh, I know that!"

And the old lady forcibly put the girl to bed; she must sleep, she must be fresh for to-morrow, she looked so pale. And then Elsa lay in bed and looked around the room, which the snowy winter night filled with a dim twilight. The dying fire flickered in the tiled stove, there stood the chest, there the doll house; it was all so indescribably cosey and homelike. And then dream and reality began to blend with each other, and she fell asleep.

It was bright day when she waked, and the sun shone into the pleasant room. It surely was filled with the fragrance of violets.

She looked about her, she could scarcely realize where she was; then she started up from the pillows. Mrs. von Ratenow sat on the edge of the bed, and gazed at her solemnly, with a huge bunch of violets in her hand.

"Good morning, you lazy Elsa!"

"Oh aunt, forgive me," stammered Elsa, in embarrassment.

"I am glad that you have come, little girl, and now give me your hand. So then, no more defiance and no more enmity, eh? She never meant unkindly, the old

aunt. You must surely know that. And now she begs
your forgiveness if she tormented and pained you. Do
you know what it means when an old woman like me
says to a chit like you, 'I beg you not to be angry
with me'?" With these words she drew the girl tenderly
toward her, and patted her cheek, while the bunch of
violets fell upon the counterpane.

"They are from the Bennewitzer, Elsa," said she.

Elsa suddenly grew very pale.

"Yes, really, Elsa! And I have a message for you
too. But dress yourself quickly ; meanwhile I will wait
in Lott's room."

With anxiously beating heart the girl dressed. No,
it was not possible, they could not be preparing a new
blow for her—oh, no ; Moritz said he had an adopted
son ; it was probably only a reconciliation with him.

Then she entered Aunt Lott's pleasant sitting-room.
"Oh, a lovely winter day ! " said the latter, pointing out
of the window.

"Just the weather for sleighing," said Mrs. von Ratenow. "How would you like to have a sleigh-ride, Elsa ?
But come now ; are you ready, Lott ? We are to breakfast together to-day, Elsa, with Moritz." And she
took the young girl's arm, and went out into the corridor with her.

"Well, I cannot help it, Elsa dear, I must tell you,"
said she, as they walked down the corridor ; "the Bennewitzer sends his most cordial greetings—the old one,
of course ; the younger dares not yet—and he promised

your father on his death-bed to care for you, shield and protect you, so he must keep his word. As you refused to be his wife, he hopes perhaps it may be more to your liking to be his daughter-in-law. But child—do not be so violent. What is the matter with you? Hold her fast, Aunt Lott!"

But that was no longer necessary. Suddenly Elsa leaned as though unconscious, against the old lady's shoulder, just as she opened the drawing-room door.

"Elsa, Elsa! She usually is so brave, and now her courage fails her. Yes, yes, the Bennewitzer's son plays the violin; he is a fine talented young fellow."

Suddenly Elsa stood alone in the beautiful room; she had clutched the back of one of the high arm-chairs, and listened with failing senses. It could not be possible! All that aunt had said, all that rang in her ears, and whispered of a wondrous, unbounded happiness— no, it could not be!

Then it ceased abruptly, the playing; and hurried, joyous footsteps came toward her, and then a voice said, "Elsa, what is happiness if it is not this hour?"

All was silence in the adjoining room. Aunt Rate-now went to the portières, drew aside the folds for a moment, and looked through. Then she turned back to the Bennewitzer; nodding gravely she gave him her hand, and both stood at the window and gazed out into the garden.

"Tic-tac, tic-tac," said the little clock; no other

sound was audible, not a word from the next room, only once a soft sob.

"Ah, well, pray show yourselves, children!" cried

Moritz at length; the time seemed unending to him. Then they came, and a girl glowing with happiness threw her arms around the Bennewitzer's neck.

" Cousin ! " she sobbed ." have you forgiven me ! You are too good, much too good to me."

" I have nothing to forgive, child," said he gently.

" How shall I thank you, cousin ? "

" By coming soon to Bennewitz, Elsa. It is so lonely there."

" She did not want me—really she did not want me ; confess it, Elsa ! " And Bernardi drew her from the Bennewitzer's arms to his breast. "She said she was only a poor girl ! "